FAUN SONG
S. A. BAKER

FAUN SONG
S. A. BAKER

Science Fiction and Fantasy Publications

HTTPS://SCIFIFANTASYPUBLICATIONS.CA
A division of DAOwen Publications

Faun Song / S. A. Baker
Edited by Douglas Owen and M. J. Moores

ISBN 978-1-928094-28-9
EISBN 978-1-92094-37-1

Jacket Art by Kayla Stumpf

10 9 8 7 6 5 4 3 2 1

To err is human, to forgive divine. To err again is worth organizing into chapters.

This book is dedicated to everyone who enjoyed the first one enough to harass me about writing this one almost immediately afterward.

ONE

"Nope." Isobel Schneider rolled onto her right side, fluttering sheets and woolen blankets briefly into the air and then back over top of her again. Then, she sighed, flipping onto her back and rolling onto her chest. She turned to her left side, and finally returned to her original position of half right side and half back. She decided nothing she would do from this point on would make any sort of real difference in her ability to sleep.

"Nope," she said again. "It's no good, no good at all."

The night air lacked the crispness it should have had for late October. The autumn moon hung nearly at ground level, brilliant and gargantuan in the sky. It cast a light across Millar's field bright enough to read by. Directly below it, not nearly as bright but still visible and casting shadow, sat a sun that should have long ago trundled off to bed and given way to the darkness. It slowly made its way past the horizon, as though suspecting the moon of having an entirely provocative time without it, and refused to go away until it was damn good and ready. It was a Wednesday night, the clock on the nightstand read 2:15 a.m. and Isobel Schneider could not sleep.

"Nope," she repeated quietly.

She rose up and moved from her bed, as silently as one could across wood floors well over a hundred years old which creaked and groaned with even the thought of movement, never mind a single footfall. If growing up here taught her anything, it was how to exit the musty old house without being discovered.

Isobel suited up in the clothes she'd stashed under her bed: an old pair of grey woolen trousers and high necked, black wool, football sweater with a red stripe running horizontally across the chest – which on closer examination, she replaced under her bed in favour of a lighter, red tartan work shirt over top of her nightshirt. They were warm and comfortable, if not a little too large and, what's more, they could hold up to the type of abuse she was liable to heap on them during nights like tonight.

Isobel had acquired the clothes from the overflowing top of an already burdened trash can after the kid across the street died. Alec Millar was the same age as she, went to the same school and shared a couple of classes with her. Apart from that, Isobel knew nothing about him. Save for the fact that he came to school with black eyes and bruises more than any other kid. If the rumours were true, the only additional thing she knew now, was he died in a pool of blood on the new carpet inside Butler's.

If she were the one who died, Isobel reasoned, she'd want her life to amount to more than all of her clothing and handful of baseball cards thrown in the trash cans by a disconsolate mother. Wearing them, she thought, gave at least some measure of proof the Millar boy had ever existed, and that gave her some hope the world wasn't an altogether a wicked place.

Isobel, unlike the boy whose clothing she currently wore, was quite small for her age, and it gave her the appearance of being a perpetual child, though she was nearly fifteen. If nothing else, the size of the clothes, particularly the length of the trousers that covered her feet entirely, would make a near silent venture into the kitchen and out the door, a near guaranteed success. Her whole life had danced perilously above the bread line, and the feeling of a full belly at bed time before Christmas, or her birthday, might just as well have been a visit from the blue fairy for all the chance of it happening. The temptation of raiding the ice box before she went out the door was nearly overwhelming and, were it not for her mother knowing where everything in the refrigerator was – down to the smallest lump of stale cheese, she might have shoved as much in her gob as she could.

She eyed the basket of old hats that had somehow always ended up back in her room, despite being moved more times than not.. Wearing one of them would do much to keep the hair out of her face but, more importantly, would do twice as much to keep the heat in and she sensed she would be too warm in her clothing tonight as it was. Her hair stretched nearly to the middle of her back, long and blonde and pin straight and she preferred to wear it in a single braid, though if she would have been allowed, in complete spite of it being decidedly boyish for the day, she likely would have cut it off altogether. Calling it unruly would have been an understatement, at times it seemed to take on a life of its own. Particularly on nights like tonight when ventured out of the house and went traipsing around Winterbourne. Isobel's eyes were as green as a raindrop on a July maple leaf and, at present, were more than a little blood shot from nearly five or six consecutive sleepless nights. They scanned the room and peered off into the darkened hallway and, when she was satisfied she was safe to go, she did.

She slung her leather ankle boots over a shoulder and crept downstairs toward the back porch, carefully avoiding the fist-sized knot hole in front of the cook stove that would scream its objection and give away her location to the rest of the house.

The girl stood facing the screen door and breathed deeply. *If anything is going to trip me up, it's this God-damned door.* She imagined her father looking just like Pa Kettle, saying, "Gotta fix that one of these days, Ma," and covered her mouth to stifle a snicker.

If you had taken the fattest and laziest snail from the garden and put it in the ice box overnight, it would still not move as slowly as Isobel opening the screen door to the back porch. She held her breath and willed the door to stay silent. It obeyed and she eased it, just as silently, closed. Isobel thought she might have made a decent burglar or sneak thief if it weren't for the overwhelming guilt she'd have over stealing. Especially from people in this town who were, for the most part, so much poorer than she.

Sitting on the cool damp grass to pull her boots on, she looked and saw the three small, brown field mice at her feet. They rubbed against her, across her hands, nipping at fingers, preventing her from tying her laces and behaving in an altogether un-mouse-like fashion.

"Knock it off," she barked, completely unfazed by them.

Isobel saw the three of them a few days before, roiling and rolling around her feet like love struck kittens. She'd shooed them away, only to have them return shortly thereafter and resume fawning all over her.

Giving in, she reached down to touch all three, reasoning there were far worse things that could have become enamoured of her, at least they weren't snakes. The three of them, in turn, began to rub against the backs of her hands as she again attempted to tie her boots. For a moment they looked like a bubbling mass of brown fur and painfully cute button eyes.

"Oh, all right then," she said, and stuck out her arm. The three mice scurried upward and settled themselves in the warmth of her shirt pocket.

Isobel resumed tying her boots, and stood facing the fallow field that bordered the back of their lot. *There's a whole life out there,* and the girl knew she wasn't going to see any of it by laying on her bed, pretending to sleep. It was a short run across Millar's field to get to Parker Street, and from there it was a block and a half to White Street and downtown Winterbourne. Though she liked to pretend the neon signs and store fronts of downtown were what she desired to see in her sleeplessness, Isobel Schneider knew where she really wanted to go was beyond the artificial glare of White Street and into the ominous, viridian darkness of Seonagh's woods.

There was something about those trees, something intangible and terrifying, yet altogether bewitching, that made Isobel certain she had to enter them. When she mentioned the idea to her mother, she was told that "proper girls don't go romping around in the forest when there is so much to be done around the home". Her mother had, clearly, never spent a single moment of her life romping anywhere, and Isobel reasoned it was her duty to make up for the total absence of romp in her mother's life by entering the woods and sucking out all the exotic marrow there was to be had.

To get to Seonagh's woods, she would have to walk Grey Hollow Road, a short span of paths that bent around the corner off White Street and backed onto Winterbourne cemetery. There were few people who'd walk Grey Hollow Road in broad daylight, never mind in the middle of the night. The place gave Isobel the willies, but the only other way into Seonagh's woods was through the back property of Winterbourne asylum, and it was locked up like a prison by this time of night. And really, the place was just as willy inducing as far as she was concerned. The girl held her breath and kept telling herself there was nothing in the dark that wasn't there in the light, and headed toward the cemetery.

TWO

Winterbourne cemetery was an outmoded old burial ground that had been around nearly as long as the town of Winterbourne itself. Some whispered about its former life as an Indian burial ground desecrated by old man Winterbourne and his descendants, but most knew that to be the revulsion and stupidity of frightened, ignorant people. Rather, it was a graveyard that had long been neglected after the town created a newer, more spacious cemetery on the other side of town. Its plots and tombstones were now so overgrown with stinging nettles, bracken and ancient oaks battered and bent by decades of late winter storms, that it had become a gnarled and nightmarish place holding little resemblance to the hallowed ground it had once been.

Isobel stood before the wrought iron gates of Winterbourne cemetery and looked to Seonagh's woods beyond. If there was an easier way to get to those woods, a less creepy, less skin-crawly way, Isobel didn't know it. What the girl did know was she had been through here dozens of times in the daylight, to pick wildflowers at the edge of the forest, and not a single thing happened to her. Neither phantasm nor devil had so much as even called her a nasty name, and good sense said nothing would happen now. But the fear of walking through a derelict, overgrown cemetery in the middle of the night rose inside and steadily thumped away at that good sense. It told her if she didn't get through this awful place quickly, something equally awful would snatch her up and do monstrous things to her before she met an untimely end.

The blonde-haired girl reached up to pull the iron ring handle on the gate and, to her surprise, it wasn't locked. She supposed cemeteries weren't the kind of place one would feel a need to break into – potentially haunted ones, even less so. The gate swung slowly and squealed conspicuously as she pulled it open. If she hoped not to arouse the spirits that might be within, that hope vanished with every loud inch of the gate's swing.

Holding her breath, Isobel walked quickly along the path that led from one end of the cemetery straight through to the other. She kept her eyes fixed on the dark outline of the forest that loomed larger on the horizon with every hasty step she took. The small girl was nearly through the ghastly place when she stopped, suddenly, intrigued by what lay beside her.

The Winterbourne family mausoleum stood at the centre of the cemetery, an obscene, imposing building, fashioned in its entirety from the finest green Peruvian marble that money could buy. Isobel had read about its construction in the school library. The quality of the marble had lost none of its sheen over the years, still reflecting the light of the full moon and dull glow of the nonchalantly setting sun in a way that gave it an almost liquid appearance. *Old man Winterbourne never did anything small.*

Standing in front of the door, the massive thing looming above her, Isobel felt as though she were back in the first grade staring up at the door to the school principal's office. She was certain no end of grief would follow if she were to walk inside the marble edifice and yet, felt a nearly uncontrollable urge to do just that. The crypt was easily the largest structure inside the old cemetery and, by all accounts, the largest building in the town itself before the Gimbel's went up on Parker Street. The tomb drew people to the town during the early nineteen hundreds – decadence of this magnitude didn't exist outside of the big cities, and here was the eighth wonder of the world just beyond downtown Winterbourne.

Isobel stood silently in front of it for a while before she heard it – a sound, barely perceptible, like the constant whine of crickets but lower in pitch like a hundred bows being drawn across the strings of a hundred thick bass fiddles, imperceptibly slow in an endless drone. She leaned her head toward the mausoleum, believing the sound originated from within it, and to her relief, she realized the sound came from in front of her, in the direction of Seonagh's woods.

Without much more thought for the mausoleum or the long dead Winterbourne's in it, Isobel headed out of the cemetery and made her way across the field of thigh-high switch grass bordering the vast glade. The nearer she got to the forest, the louder the droning became. When she got within a hundred feet of the trees, she noticed it wasn't a steady drone at all. It was voices, many of them singing as one, in tones that rose and fell but never strayed from the melody of the whole.

Isobel felt the icy fingers of blind dread tingle across the back of her neck, but was so mesmerized, so taken by the song, that she seemed guided by it straight into the depth of the emerald dark.

She moved closer to the grove and caught a glimpse of what looked like a child wearing a red waistcoat standing just in front of the trees, staring at her with eyes transfixed and mouth agape, frozen in place. As she got a better look at him, she could see a chestnut coloured, neatly trimmed, full beard lining his chin. Their eyes met and a look of panic crossed the little man's face before he broke his gaze and disappeared into the shadow of the copse.

The girl darted toward the tree line after the smaller being, but stopped short when the monstrous fear inside her reared up and cautioned her against proceeding any farther into the glade. She reached out her arms, and moved slowly toward the massive box elders that rimmed the outside of Seonagh's woods. Isobel was almost close enough to touch them when she noticed a deer fly land on her forearm. Swatting it away only caused it to be replaced by two more that quickly settled where the first had been and began to dine. Soon they were joined by a dozen of their friends.

The faster the girl swatted the loathsome things away, the faster they came back, and in greater numbers. Soon, Isobel was covered by them, thousands of black-winged, caustic emissaries from the profane forest that completely overwhelmed and drove her face first to the turf. She knew if she continued to lie in one place, the deer flies would strip her bones bare in short order, so she summoned what little strength remained and pushed herself up from the cold wetness. Isobel limped toward Winterbourne cemetery, swatting and shooing the deerflies off of her as she went.

She reached the back gates and pushed through them, collapsing at the foot of the mausoleum. As quickly as it had begun, the assault had ceased without so much as a single deerfly sticking around for second helpings of the girl's blood.

"God-damn," she breathed, and immediately covered her mouth, calling to mind an exasperated mother and the all-consuming anger that would issue forth at the thought of that kind of language leaving Isobel's mouth. Her mind flashed suddenly to a horrid image of three small brown mice, crushed gruesomely inside of the shirt pocket they'd crawled into earlier and lifted the flap to peer in on them. Instead, she found them not mangled or broken, but sleeping soundly and looking desperately adorable doing so.

The light of the autumn moon had begun to wane slowly in the direction of the horizon, and had given way to a brief measure of blackness that Isobel felt surprisingly calmed by. Neither the calm nor the darkness lasted long as the first traces of daylight ripped their way, like a gruesome, jagged wound opened across the throat of an otherwise bucolic moment. Soon the dawn oozed through, crimson and ocher and pooling on the grass at the bottom of the trees like the night's lifeblood. It was as early in the morning as it could possibly be, and Isobel Schneider was no nearer to sleep than she had been when she left the house. She was sure however, that the second her head hit the pillow, that would all change and a glorious slumber would come to her. A full-on panic took hold of her and reality crammed its way into her mind. She was uncertain of the time but knew her mother would be up already, likely since long before the rising of the sun, and already fuming over having to throw in her lot with a shiftless husband and a daydreaming daughter. And if Isobel did not rise from the indolent comfort of her bed precisely when told to do so, there would be no end of hell to pay.

THREE

The sun pushed is way past the laggard, russet moon and over the gnarled and bent tops of the pear trees that lined the yard of the Schneider home. It was early Saturday morning, and Ezra Schneider took a cautious sip of his coffee and lit up his first Chesterfield. *Best time of the day.* His wife and daughter, along with the rest of the town of Winterbourne, still slept. Nobody wanted anything from him, and there was nothing more to the world than the smell of fresh coffee, the hot sting of his first cigarette and the almost sickly-sweet odour of fallen pears rotting merrily away on the front lawn.

Ezra sucked in as much air as his lungs would allow, threw his head back, and let the enormous breath out slowly enough to make himself feel a little light headed. He took a healthy sized puff of his Chesterfield and blew it out equally as slow. It was a good day to be on the front porch. Sure, there were things to do, little things like lawn cutting and he was certain his wife had a list as long as his right leg of things that needed done. But here, right here, right now, in the cool early morning air, it was a great time to simply be, and Ezra was fully prepared to do just that.

As he took another sip of his coffee, the man noticed the small figure he'd been casually observing, become larger, and move, determinedly, toward him. He continued to sit, without concern for the figure, drinking his coffee, and smoking his Chesterfield.

"That looks like my daughter Isobel, but it can't be. My daughter Isobel is fast asleep in her bed upstairs."

"Dada, I can explain."

"I seriously God-damn doubt it," Ezra snapped, and after a moment, and another drag from his Chesterfield, softened his tone. "Not well enough for your mother, anyway."

"Is Mother awake?" A tone of dread raised in her voice.

"For some time now, and been looking for you, almost since she got up. You better go in and see what she wants." He stared at her, waiting for some kind of sign to register on her face.

Isobel stood at the foot of the stairs and felt the life drain out of her. Her mother would have a great deal to say about her daughter not being immediately available the second she opened her eyes, and none of it pleasant. She climbed up the stone steps, head hanging, feet dragging in defeat. The girl wished she would have, even for a moment, considered staying home and hoped her mother wasn't nearly angry enough to do something crazed like locking her inside her room for the better part of a whole day – again.

Ezra's arm shot out, preventing Isobel from walking past him.

"Wait," he began. "Take this." He handed her a rolled-up newspaper. "I told your mother the paper boy forgot us again and that I sent you out to find him and get me the morning paper."

A smile of exhausted relief leaped across Isobel's face and she felt the weight of panic evaporate from her shoulders.

"Dada!" She threw her arms around his neck, hugging him for all she was worth.

"Look it," said Ezra. "We're going to talk about this later, you and me. I want to know where you're going and why, okay?"

"Okay."

She changed quickly out of the woollen trousers and red tartan work shirt, and carefully replaced them in the Gimbel's hat box under her bed, making certain her three travelling companions had left before she put the lid on. They were gone, but she couldn't for the life of her recall feeling them leave her pocket. They may have been unlike any mice she'd ever seen before, but they were still mice after all, and if left to their own devices with her nice wool shirt, it would be nice wool rags within a few hours.

Isobel remembered seeing the elaborate, Sunday go-to-meeting hat in the window of the department store coming home from school one day, and begged her parents to buy it for her. Promising no end of chores and a complete cessation of all tomfoolery forthwith, but the girl knew her parents could never afford such an extravagance as a brand-new hat – one costly enough to come in a box. She dropped the subject after its first mentioning, heartbroken and knowing the answer before the words left her lips. Some days later, she arrived home from school to find a hat box on her bed. The box contained a note from her father which read: Nothing ever came from a dream you gave up on. One hat to follow. Her heart had lifted after reading it and she stashed the box under her bed for fear of her mother finding it and questioning and berating her father about its origins and cost.

She returned to the kitchen and stood before her mother, who stood at the stove, back to the world.

"Um," Isobel began.

"Yes?" her mother snapped.

"I'm back."

"Fascinating,"

Confused by this exchange, Isobel moved again to the back porch to find her father. He had not moved from his previous position in the chair, legs crossed and resting on the wooden rail. Ezra drained his coffee, sparked up a fresh Chesterfield, and smiled at Isobel.

"Well, what have you to say for yourself?"

"I, um…" Isobel was never quite sure how to take her father. His bearing was, generally, that of someone hanging on the ragged edge. With only the slightest jostling needed to push him over the edge completely.

"That wood is not going to cut itself," Ezra said, his tone ringing with annoyance.

"No Dada."

They walked down the porch steps in silence and crossed the yard toward the enormous stump they used for wood cutting.

"Sonofabitch," Ezra said.

"What?" Isobel asked, a little worried for what the answer might be.

"This God-damned wood *isn't* going to cut itself." His voice suddenly softened.

Ezra looked at her, and a broad smile stretched its way across his eyes long before it followed on his lips. Isobel sighed, and smiled back at him.

"Language, Dada," she mockingly scolded.

"Aww, she can't hear us from here."

Isobel pulled the axe from the stump, and picked up one of the split logs from the pile beside it. She cleaved it easily, and her father replaced it with another as quickly as she had split the first. They went on like this, in silence, for an uncomfortable amount of time before Ezra broke the tension.

"Are you really going to make me ask?"

"Do you really want to know?"

"You know damn well I do."

"You know where I went, Dada."

"Why? What is it about that bastarding place that makes you keep going back?"

"Would you believe me if I said I didn't know? Would you believe that I can't explain why, but I know I just have to get into Seonagh's woods?"

"Most wouldn't," Ezra said after several silent minutes. "Most would say you're off your God-damn nut, and your mother and I should lock you up in Winterbourne and forget about you. But I know better. I felt the same way no matter how much my parents whipped me, and they did. I kept trying to go back into that awful bastarding forest. I just felt like I had to get into it."

"Why, Dada?" Isobel said, slightly incredulous at finding out that her father understood the compulsion that kept her awake at night.

"I wish I could tell you. I couldn't ever get closer than a hundred feet of those God-damned trees."

"Too frightened?" A swell of pride for having nearly touched one of the trees.

"Too many God-damned deer flies!" Ezra said. "Those evil shitting things chewed my ass raw!"

"Dada!" she exclaimed in mock surprise at the saltiness of his language. Though, in reality, it would have bothered her more if he hadn't spoken the way he did. Isobel felt as if the weight of the world had just been lifted off her shoulders. She wasn't going crazy, and it would seem, she wasn't the only Schneider who felt the need to go off willingly into the place that filled everyone else with a creeping fear.

"Look." her father said as he pushed away the split pieces of wood and replaced it with another small log. "I won't tell you to not go in there - I doubt you'd listen if I did. But know this, if your mother finds out you're going in there and you tell her that you don't know why but you have to keep going, daughter or not, I don't think she'd think twice about locking you up in a room at the top of the hill and throwing away the God-damned key."

Ezra put down the log and embraced his daughter, looking her in the eye.

"I don't pretend that I understand what it is about that assing place that puts the hooks into us so bad, but I have a feeling you have to go into it. Like maybe something terrible will happen if you don't. I still feel like I have to sometimes, and it scares the shit out of me. Just promise me two things."

"What, Dada?" Isobel felt a tear roll down her cheek.

"First, if you make it in there, past the deer flies, I want to know exactly what's in there."

"And second?"

"That you swear to me you'll come back out of the God-damned place if you can."

FOUR

The large room reeked of incense and the ancient, perpetually damp wood, rose in thick panels all the way up to form the apex of the vaulted ceiling. At the head of the room stood an altar fashioned from three equally great slabs of grey granite. Draped over the makeshift stone altar, like a single drop of blood, was a strip of the finest red Chinese silk. The whole thing was bathed in a kaleidoscopic.

Diffused light streamed in through high windows that adorned the walls of the great hall. Above this colourful display hung the figure of a man, though gilded and clearly revered, obviously in the midst of untold suffering.

Father Winslow Brennan bent low before the altar of the punished man, and touched his head to the floor in reverence.

"My lord. I am humbly sorry for having offended thee."

He made the sign of the cross against his chest, stood to his full height, and moved to the small anteroom that lay to the left of the altar. His lips bent into a wry, knowing smile. It wasn't as though he believed any of this sacrosanct rigmarole – he didn't.

He had seen more things in this world and enough glimpses into the next to tell him there was no almighty, forgiving father waiting to clutch us to his bosom in the great by and by. The priest knew perfectly well from the things he had done himself, that if there was any sort of beneficent deity, it didn't give a shit about any of us, much less care about punishing the wicked. Because the Right Reverend Father Winslow Brennan, had been wicked –

wickeder than a dozen men who'd lived twice as long, and he had positively no interest in stopping now.

The priest unbuttoned his collar and removed his cassock, leaving him in plain black trousers and a white t-shirt. He kicked off his leather soled shoes in favour of a well worn pair of basketball shoes and pulled on a black, wool cardigan as he walked to his study. Standing before the sturdy bookshelves that lined the walls, he remarked that his life's journey would surely begin, and end, within the pages of ancient texts. Though, he suspected, two very different ones.

The priest searched for the precise mouldering volume that would answer the question that had burned in his mind all day, and when it appeared, after a concerted effort to lay hands on it, he wrest it from between two equally cumbersome books. At his desk, he sat and put his feet up.

It was a massive book by all standards, bound in some type of leather. Most who glimpsed the book believed it to be human skin, though there was no real proof of it. And, all were fairly certain the writings within it must be arcane and eldritch, containing spells and rituals to bring about the end of the world. But most who thought these things had spent their lifetimes looking at movie magazines and Reader's Digest, and thought no actual good could ever come from a proper book.

Winslow Brennan wasn't interested in any of those types of books, ancient and evil, or otherwise. The Right Reverend and Venerated Father wanted information. The book he held, the leather bound ancient and strange text was titled *The Celebrated and Annotated History of the town of Winterbourne*. Which goes to show that looking isn't always seeing.

It had been written in 1810, two years after old man Winterbourne had claimed the large strip of an onion field as his own and built a textile mill that employed most of the town. So, when he had decided he wanted to build a home befitting the family of a man of his fiscal standing and sway with the town, nobody objected when the gothic manor house with five spires was built atop the hill overlooking the entire town.

The old man had insisted the town change its name to Winterbourne, in recognition of all he'd done for it, and the town relented. When he threatened to clear cut Seonagh's woods however, a place the townsfolk had regarded with unease and healthy respect, they assured him they would burn him out of his castle and out of town regardless of how much money he had. And there it ended, for a time anyway, but old man Winterbourne was given to fits of madness and began to believe that something was living in that forest and therefore, on his land. He decreed he would raze that damnable copse to the ground by axe or sword or flame and evict whatever lived off of his good graces permanently. Or, at the very least, collect an enormous amount of back rent.

Father Brennan flipped through the pages and read about the mundane events of a small town through the ages, of fairs and pie eating contests, of newly crowned Corn Queens and businesses opening and closing, and not another word was written about old man Winterbourne until near the end of the book's records. There, firstly, was a photograph of him holding a small, vaguely human shaped statue with the caption *Artefacts in Seonagh's woods?* and *Silver?* Beside the photo was a small caption relating the madness that had plagued old man Winterbourne for so many years and had finally taken its toll as the night before he had taken leave of his senses, and set light to the manor house, presumably with himself and his family within it.

"Hmm," Father Brennan said.

He got up, and went to the locked cupboard on the other side of the dais. The priest inserted the small brass key into the receiver and removed a two-foot-high statue. It was a likeness of the God Pan, bronze and gilt in spots, reclining on the stump of a tree. At the foot of the statue rested a small tin placard reading; 'Graciously donated by the estate of Mr. A. H. Winterbourne.' Father Brennan thought *graciously donated* seemed like an awfully nice way of saying stolen from the estate a man who went mad, killed himself, and all of his living heirs.

The cleric picked up the statue and felt the surprising weight of it. The craftsmanship was impeccable, and it would make a fine addition to anyone's collection. He turned the statue and saw the underside of the base seemed to be silver. On closer inspection, he found there were several small spots of wear on the bronze that also shone through silver. He removed a small pen knife from the pocket of his cardigan and scraped at the back of the statue. The whole thing seemed to be made of fine silver painted to look like bronze. The priest bent down, examined the cupboard, and found a small decal reading "Senoagh's woods?"

Father Brennan examined the statue further, and when he was convinced there were no more secrets to be found on it, placed it back in the cupboard. As he did, a small scrap of very old and much yellowed paper caught his eye. Written on it was a rhyme that had become nauseatingly familiar since arriving in this town. One of his superiors had recited it after telling him he was being transferred to Winterbourne.

> *Don't dawdle foolish child and do as you are told*
> *Stay clear of ancient names and trees both bent and bowed.*
> *Don't tempt fate by whistling and never curse the cold*
> *For Death stalks the halls of Winterbourne house*
> *And the Devil walks Grey Hollow Road.*

FIVE

Isobel walked slowly toward the back porch and her waiting mother. She wanted to walk quickly, knowing full-well that the more time it took to get there, the more likely the woman would blow her stack before she arrived at the porch. Sometimes, she would meander across the yard on purpose, just to watch the old girl go crazy with frustration. This however, was not one of those times.

Her mother grunted disapprovingly and pushed the overflowing wicker laundry basket toward Isobel with her foot, before thrusting out a large tin can full of clothes pegs.

"When you've finished with these, you can get started on the breakfast dishes while you explain to me where you really were this morning," her mother said.

The younger of the two women silently acknowledged, and began to tug and poke at the wet clothing, stringing it over the wash line until her mother disappeared into the house.

Isobel tried desperately to keep her attention on the back porch and hands on the heavy wet clothes, but her mind had other plans and was now walking gracefully and slowly along Grey Hollow road, approaching the cemetery gates with a father whom she'd only just learned was once as adventurous as her. The girl smiled, picturing him looking down at her as they walked past the Winterbourne family mausoleum in the bright light of day. Father and daughter heading nonchalantly out the back gates, and straight into Seonagh's woods. But, one foot into the trees and she heard an uncomfortable snap, and the world of trees fell away.

Isobel's mother stood face to face with her. She snapped her fingers again, and brought a quick flat hand against the side of her daughter's head with the force of a Roman candle.

"Where are you, girl?" her mother bellowed. "Bootless shirk-a-day that you are. Not anywhere near this laundry, that's for certain."

Isobel came out of her stupor just in time to see the overfilled clothesline snap, and the freshly washed shirts fall into the dark earth of the vegetable garden.

Ezra rose from his seat across the porch from his daughter, biting his lip as hard as he could – nearly hard enough to draw blood. Try as he might, he could not ebb the belly laugh that bubbled up through him. It flew out and doubled him over in ebullient fits beside the wood pile.

"Well," Ezra said, stifling the laughter and trying to sound as serious as he possibly could. "It's never good to have too much free time."

The laughter resumed and he was, once again, near to falling down in hysterics.

Isobel gathered up the clothes in embittered silence and headed back indoors to the dank, musty basement where the Speed Queen washer held court. The girl looked around at the cobweb-covered, bare, stone walls as she stuffed the muddied clothes into the wash tub feeling cold and isolated and alone.

"Cripes," she said. "It's no wonder she's always mad."

The blonde girl came up from the basement and headed back outside the house, being careful to avoid making noise anywhere close to the kitchen, where she was certain her mother currently still stewed and seethed and spent no undue amount of time thinking up ways to make her daughter miserable. She walked around the back of the house toward the wood pile, hoping to find her father there and ask him something, anything, about what he knew of Seonagh's woods.

Isobel caught a flash of movement out of the corner of her eye and looked left of the rows of cord wood, toward the storm cellar. Her heart thundered under her mud stained, white pinafore as she moved slowly toward the movement. It wasn't fear necessarily, though if it were a skunk or a rabid raccoon, she was fairly certain there would be a scream and a quick sprint in the other direction. But the storm cellar was a place that never failed to frighten, and even thinking of walking past it sent cold fear crawling up her collar like an obscene lizard.

She walked silently toward the Bilco doors, her heart pounding in her chest. Isobel stepped close enough to touch one of the long, heavy, steel doors and wanted to open one and hurry inside to the safety of the basement, but stopped short when she saw three, small, brown field mice rolling around and chasing each other across the concrete pilings that held the doors in place.

"Really?" she panted. "Really? I nearly wet myself."

The three mice stopped dead and looked up at her through identical sets of coal black eyes, noses twitching expectantly. The smallest of them broke away from the huddle and scuttled nervously toward Isobel's boot, lowering itself into as non-threatening a position as is possible for a field mouse.

"Oh, for the love of… come here then."

She bent down to allow the mouse to climb into her hand when she heard it. A voice, tiny and nearly imperceptible, but at the same time, it shook through her ears like a clap of thunder rattling the windows of her bedroom.

"Come closer," the voice said.

She heard one of the Bilco doors groan awfully and pop open; she took a fearful step backward.

"Not that way," the voice said.

The right storm door swung up and open, landing with a deafening, heavy, metal clang.

A cool breeze, thick with dust and the smell of several lifetimes of neglect, rose up to meet her as she peered in through the door to the darkened room below.

"I feared not the darkness until I first saw the light," the voice breathed.

"What?" Isobel said.

"I'm sorry?" the voice said.

"I said what – As in what does that mean, exactly?"

"Oh, well…" the voice sputtered. "It means that you should…"

"Yes?" Isobel now sounding slightly annoyed.

"Look, could you just come down the stairs, please?"

Coin sized spears of light filtering through holes in the dust-caked windows and threw just enough light for Isobel to find the switch on the hanging bulb in the centre of the room. She turned it. The bulb flickered and slowly glowed to its fullest, dull orange illumination, revealing a room she felt may have been best left in the dark. Isobel couldn't believe anything would want to be down here among the cobwebs and ancient dust, never mind why an otherworldly voice would practically insist she come down the stairs. The thought of trying to find the source of the voice or it's reason for her being in the basement in all of this grime, was nearly enough to make her turn back up the stairs and slam the Bilco doors behind her.

There were many large piles of oily, dank tarpaulin covered boxes spread out over the length and breadth of the entire room. Along the back wall sat an imposing and hardy looking wooden work bench, also full of long forgotten boxes. Isobel picked through one or two of them and found things she couldn't imagine anyone purchasing ever, let alone missing if they weren't in immediate view.

When the boxes yielded no answers - no voice nor its reason for calling her, she turned to move on from the work bench, when she spied a small, ornate wooden chest no bigger than her mother's jewelry box that had a fine copper escutcheon plate on the front of it. The box wasn't locked, and it opened easily, revealing a handful of old photographs and a small picture key chain that read "Greetings from Coney Island".

The keychain held a picture of a handsome looking woman and two youngish boys, all standing arm in arm in front of a banner proclaiming one of the wonders of the modern world was there in the flesh. Isobel couldn't be certain just what the wonder was; the figures in the picture obscured the rest of the sign.

She stared at the keychain with a fair degree of certainty that one of these boys was her father. Even as a dark-haired boy, his face held the same stern and slightly chafed look that belied his generally convivial nature. And, as she imagined her father didn't spring up from the ground or hatch from an egg, the girl felt fairly safe in assuming the woman with him was his mother.

But who was the other boy in the picture? Isobel had never heard him mention a brother before, though he'd never mentioned his fondness for hard liquor and pickled eggs on Friday nights, and there was little doubt about that. She thumbed through the stack of pictures and, after reasonably investigating them, laid three of them out in a straight line on the dusty wooden bench. Her three travelling companions scurried suddenly out of the darkness and began pushing the small wooden box toward her.

"Jesus!" she yelped, and pushed the box back away emphatically. Her hand moved to cover her mouth, picturing her mother admonishing such an outburst. "No, I have all of the pictures I need, thank you."

The three mice were undeterred, however, and pushed it back to her with a force she didn't think possible from them.

"No, really you three, I don't want it."

The smallest of the three crawled inside the box and glowered up at her with a look that was the nearest to "Have a look inside this box you cloth-eyed twit." as a small, painfully cute, brown field mouse could get.

25

"What?" Isobel sighed and pulled the mouse out of the box.

She was confronted by an image of herself, though a considerably younger version. Suddenly a vague recollection of sitting in front of a strange man with an even stranger puppet and a good deal of talk about watching a bird that never did seem to make an appearance danced through her head. The blue-eyed girl laid her own photo alongside the other three and was startled to see breathtaking similarities. Of course there were the obvious differences between males and females that go without saying, but the eyes, those icy, pallid eyes almost devoid of life and emotion. Isobel thought if she covered all of the photos, leaving only the eyes visible, she would be hard-pressed to tell which was which.

Where the photo had been, hiding in the shadows of the small box, lay a scrap of folded paper barely perceptible in the grimy recesses of the small, aged coffin. Isobel opened the folds and saw it was a newspaper clipping.

Bodies found near Seonagh's woods!

The bodies of a woman and child were found on the Winterbourne estate late Wednesday evening by the groundskeepers. The bodies have been identified as Mrs. Elsie Schneider and her eldest child, Ira. Both appear to have been dispatched by repeated blows with a blunt object. Mrs. Schneider's husband and her remaining child still, as yet, unaccounted for. The local constabulary remain vigilant and confident that they will get to the truth in this matter in short order.

"Murdered?"

"Your family has always been unique," the voice returned.

"What?"

"A long time have we watched your family. Powerful people one and all."

"Powerful people?" Isobel wondered aloud, intrigued by the syrupy – sweet voice.

"Yesssss," the voice hissed, its words dipping with deliciously crushing, seductive honey. "Powerful. In time, the destiny of your line will change the fate of the world."

Isobel turned in the direction she supposed the voice came from.

"Yessss," the voice hissed again. "And you, my child, will be the *most* powerful of your line."

Isobel felt certain it was the same voice she first heard on the outside of the Bilco doors, but changed now, full of a sinister and sickly-sweet quality that became too hard to resist. Her feet began walking forward with little prompting from her mind, toward the other end of the storm cellar which seemed to be lengthening as she walked.

The three small mice began thrashing around the girl's feet and crawling up her boots, nipping at bare ankles in an effort to stop the unconscious movement forward, but the voice had cast out its silken line and set the hook deep.

"Yesssss my child." It reeled her in.

Isobel felt herself stumbling forward faster now, and soon felt no control over her actions, as though she floated along like a balloon on a summer breeze. At the end of the elongated storm cellar wall, stood a large double door, bathed in a deep emerald glow. The bewitched young girl suddenly heard the low visceral singing of a hundred thousand, impossibly deep voices buzz around her head like so many fat, happy bees, and felt herself unable to resist the call. She closed her eyes and stretched her arms out to the waiting glow.

The smallest of the brown field mice ran along the stout legs of the dusty work bench until it reached the top. It followed a length of rope tied to the wall near the top of the bench that supported a large crate hanging just above the concrete wall Isobel hypnotically headed toward. The other two soon joined it in gnawing for all they were worth, in the hopes of bringing the large crate down.

Isobel felt the door swing open, saw the lush green trees beyond it and felt herself let go of any desire to stay in the stygian, musty storm cellar. A sudden crash from behind broke the spell, and her feet hit the ground, turning immediately to where she had stood.

She looked at remnants of the broken crate that covered the floor where she'd been standing, and watched the olive glow of the doors fade and disappear back into the shabby cobwebbed walls of the storm cellar. The dreamy voice cleared out, her wits returned to her slowly, and Isobel looked down to see the three brown field mice rolling around her feet.

"What the…" she sputtered.

"What the hell are you doing down here?" Ezra bellowed.

SIX

Father Brennan sat at the far corner of the bar inside Butler's and lit a fresh cigarette. He picked up the glass in front of him and examined its amber contents before tilting it to his lips and draining it.

"I'll take another one of those," he said to the barman.

"Father, ain't it wrong for a priest to be drinking?" the barman wondered.

"Only if you take a vow of vice, my son," Father Brennan said. He made the sign of a cross in the air and emptied the glass the barman placed in front of him. "Hit me again."

The barman shrugged his shoulders and reached for the whisky.

"How long have you lived in Winterbourne, Karl?"

"Me, I'm a native. My great-grandparents were some of the original settlers. Why do you ask?"

"What can you tell me about Seonagh's woods?"

"That creepy place? I can tell you to stay the hell away from it."

"Why?" The priest stared through the whisky as he swirled it in the bottom of his glass. "What is everyone so afraid of up there?"

"Don't you know the rhyme?"

"Of course I know it," Brennan spat. "I don't think there's anyone in this town who doesn't know that stupid thing."

"It's not as stupid as you might think. There's a lot of truth in it."

"Are you telling me that you actually believe the Devil, Satan himself, walks along the edges of Seonagh's woods?"

"You don't believe in the Devil, do you father?"

The question caught Brennan a little off guard and he sputtered and choked on a mouthful of whisky.

"Do I believe that there is one supreme, evil overlord who controls a vast army of heinous minions who spend all of eternity waiting for the strength of men to falter so they can move in to possess their immortal souls because they, themselves, are bereft of such a precious commodity? I think that's all horseshit."

"Not a very reverend attitude for a man of the cloth, Father," Karl said.

"It's a very practical attitude for a man," the priest said. "I'm a man of flesh and blood, Karl. The same as you or anyone else. I believe that evil exists in the world because men are inherently so. Not because some cloven-hoofed boogeyman made me do it."

"Made you do what exactly, Father?" Karl said, leaning in close to the priest.

"It's just an expression Karl," Brennan said, trying to deflect the bartender's question. "Can I get another?"

Karl turned back to the bar for the bottle while Brennan lit another cigarette.

"They're mild, yet they' satisfy." Brennan exhaled. "What did old man Winterbourne want in those woods?"

He turned his attention from the whisky in his hand to the quiet, grubby man behind the bar who couldn't be bothered to look back.

"Did you hear me Karl?"

Karl eyed the priest with a distrust that grew the more he looked at him. From the neatly combed hair and perfect complexion, to the smug little smile the cleric kept flashing after he ordered his drink. It may have been just an expression but, there was something unsettling about Father Brennan. And something altogether creepy. What kind of priest smoked and drank like a sailor?

"Old man Winterbourne was as crazy as a shit-house rat," Karl said. "Nobody knows where the idea came from, but he stomped around town one day shouting about treasure right in the middle of Seonagh's woods. Treasure for Christ's sake, have you ever heard anything so screwy?"

"Why did he think that?" the priest asked, sitting up with interest aroused by what the barman was about to say.

"He claimed he had found some statue in there, some silver thing. Claimed he found it at some shrine in the middle of the forest and that there was a ton more silver in there. Claimed it all belonged to him because the forest was on his land – the land that he didn't pay a single cent for, I might add."

Had he been a smarter man, Father Brennan might have stopped there, with Karl's attention moderately piqued but not enough to pry further into the priest's business. Though he was not necessarily a stupid man, Father Winslow Brennan was a very greedy man, and the potential for vast sums of wealth, even those hidden in a forest that terrified an entire town, was too strong of an enticement to leave alone.

"What do you think, Karl?"

"I think he found something in there all right, and he went off his nut because of it. Something that didn't want to be found, and something that didn't want him or anyone else in that forest. He was never quite right after he came out of that place."

"Really?"

"Really. When I was a kid, the old folks were always telling us to stay away from that place, that it would change us and not for the better. They said that time and reason were different inside the trees and there'd be a reckoning once we came back out. They tried to scare us by saying that old man Winterbourne went in there three or four times and aged five years every time he came out. Of course, us kids all just thought it was the kind of superstitious nonsense adults always use to keep children from having fun."

"But?"

"But a boy went missing the summer I turned twelve. I didn't know him well, we went to the same school but that was about the extent of it. He was gone about a year, maybe a little longer. Jesus, he was twelve. It still bothers me to think about it," Karl said.

"What, did he die in there?"

"No, he didn't die. But…"

"But what Karl?"

"But maybe he should have, I'm sure he wished he had. That kid was twelve when he went into Seonagh's woods, he came back out of the trees a twenty-five-year-old man.

"You had me up til then," Brennan sneered.

"Believe what you want Father, but I saw him. I saw how the town shunned him like a shit stained leper, I watched while his parents disowned him and he went mad with guilt and shame and trying to figure out just what the hell happened to him. In his head, he was still twelve."

"What happened to him?"

"Oh, the same thing that happened to anybody that acted a little off back then. They locked his ass away up the hill and he hanged himself with his bed sheets when he couldn't take it anymore," Karl answered.

"Did he ever say anything to anybody about what was in there? Like was there any –"

"Say, why is a priest so interested in that place anyway?" Karl said, cutting him off.

"It's purely academic," the priest lied. "I'd like to know more of the history of our fair town, and I can't seem to get the truth out of any of the books I've read. Just glossed over versions of it."

Karl threw Father Brennan a knowing, skeptical look. He was a big man who smelled of smoke and stale beer, and whose chosen occupation and manner of speech did little to dissuade people from thinking he was as dumb as ditch water. If being a barman had taught Karl anything, it was knowing when to speak, and when to remain silent. It also gave him the uncanny ability to smell a lie a mile away.

The meaty bartender poured a generous whisky and slid it toward the priest.

"I didn't order that," Brennan said.

"It's on the house," Karl said. "I want you to drink that and then I want you to leave. You're up to something and I don't want to know what it is. I imagine that look in your eyes is the same look old man Winterbourne had just before he busted his wife's head open with the fireplace poker."

Father Brennan rose from his barstool, raised the glass of whisky to his lips, and drained the liquid in one long, slow gulp, never once taking his eyes off of Karl.

"I think you have been sampling from the top shelves, Karl. That or you watch too many movies."

The priest got back to the rectory and made his way to the side door of the church, and onto the dais, fumbling, drunkenly for the keys in his pocket and promptly dropping them to the red carpeted floor. After several, clumsy, giggly attempts to pick them up without much success, he managed to retrieve the small, antique, steel keys and open the cupboard with no further delays.

Brennan picked up the statue, and looked into its eyes. Perhaps it wasn't Pan after all, but Mephistopheles himself.

"Do you really walk along Grey Hollow road?"

SEVEN

Isobel lay on top of her bed, not sleeping, the day's events twisting around like a hot knife stuck deep inside her belly.

"That voice," she said.

The voice had said in sickly sweet tones her family was powerful, powerful enough to shape the destiny of the world, and she would be...

"The mossst powerful," she breathed.

She slithered quietly from under her covers, slipped on her scratchy wool bathrobe, and grabbed the hat box from under the bed. Isobel stood gazing out the window toward the moonlit backyard and looked back, if only for a second, at her bed.

"Most Powerful," the voice rattled around in her head as she silently crept out of the bedroom.

Quietly the girl inched past the bedroom door and made her way downstairs, grabbing her Wellington boots out of the front hall closet as she passed it. The layout of the cellar would still be as unfamiliar as it had been earlier, and she knew finding the pull chain for the light in the middle of a darkened room was all but an impossibility.

Isobel remembered her mother kept a box of white candles in the cupboard just above the kitchen sink, and took three of the longest for good measure, reaching on tip toe to put the box back. As she did, the kitchen's wood floor gave a loud, resounding creak that echoed through the silent house as though the wood suddenly realized it had not been such a giving tree after all, and having bits cut away from you was an incredibly nasty and painful business.

Isobel froze in terror. Her mother could hear a cricket fart in her sleep, and a noise of this dreadful magnitude wouldn't escape her. She could feel the cold prickle of anxious flop sweat wiggle its way across a forehead already wrinkled by wide-eyed fear. Isobel knew that in the absolute best case, Ezra would be down the stairs and tell her to go back to bed after a few dour looks and some half-hearted consternations followed by a slightly confused smile. Or that, in the worst case, it would be her mother and a lecture of varying length on the evils of not doing as proper girls should, would arrive on swift and terrible wings. Likely followed by a sharp clout up the back of her head.

The frightened girl remained rooted to the spot, not sure what to do. Leaving would further enrage a mother already furious at a daughter who did not stay to get what was coming to her and staying, well… she would get what was coming to her. After what could only have been several lifetimes' passing, no one came.

Isobel looked at the big white-faced Westclox above the cook stove and reckoned it had been a full ten minutes since the floor belched out its awful death throes, and nobody had come running to investigate. She smiled a wide, triumphant smile, like the cat who ate the canary and then had the mouse and the gold fish for tea, and slowly opened the kitchen door.

Silently she crossed the backyard, save for the sucking and squelching sounds of sockless feet in rubber boots walking across dew covered grass, and arrived at the Bilco doors. Three small, furry chaperones ran out from under the shrubs and did their best to spread out across the width of the doorway.

"Not now," she said curtly.

"Squeak," the three replied.

It wasn't as though they were speaking in some form of common tongue, they weren't, but she seemed, suddenly, to have very little trouble understanding what they were trying to say.

"I have to get in there," she said, and pushed the three of them aside.

The three pushed back, as hard as they were able, squeaking their disapproval, and the smallest stood full upright on its hind legs, thinking the sudden increase in height might make it seem fierce and terrifying and altogether less mousey. Looking back at Isobel, he saw less than the desired effect on her face.

"How can it be dangerous, it's a storm cellar?"

The mice squeaked.

"Dragons?" she said. "Are you mad?"

The three looked back and forth at each other and likely would have shrugged their tiny, furry shoulders if they had some idea of how to do such.

"You heard the voice," she said. "My family has always been powerful and I will be–"

Her words stopped mid-sentence and she turned her attention to the Bilco doors as the three mice were suddenly bathed in a murky, emerald glow erupting from the void between the two doors. Isobel found her mind immediately focused on a huge, flame spitting reptile lurking just beyond the door and took a concerned step backward.

"This is not a story," she said, trying to reassure herself. "This is Winterbourne, nothing exciting ever happens in this town."

A loud, low, and far off sound like distant thunder echoing off the face of a remote mountain side rumbled behind the doors, sounding exactly as she imagined a large dragon locked behind a set of Bilco doors might sound.

"There are NO dragons," Isobel said, becoming angry with herself for even entertaining such a foolish notion. The sound came again, and the three mice ran squeaking from their picket at the foot of the door and huddled together near her feet. She stuck out a hand and they crawled up the woollen arm and nestled into the pocket of her robe.

"No, I don't think it's a cat," she said calmly.

Isobel gingerly set her hatbox down and stretched out a hand to grab one of the handles, surprised by the warmth. It wasn't hot, but nor was it as cold as a metal door handle should be in the middle of a fall night. It seemed to her something unseen, some gigantic force, held the doors shut. No matter how hard she pulled, one, and then the other, or both together, they refused to budge more than an inch or two. She felt the wriggle of the mice as they emerged from the pocket of her bathrobe. Hearing the squeaks coming from them, that she swore were dripping with sarcasm, they sauntered down the arm of her robe and settled on the ground.

"Really?" she spat. "Really, you don't think I would have thought of that first?"

She examined the doors closely and felt the wave of heat hit and quickly spread across her face as she reached up and slid back the bolt holding them firmly shut. Sheepishly, she lifted the door and found the set of concrete stairs, completely devoid of dragons, but still illuminated in the same earthy, green light.

Isobel heard the deep rumble again and it seemed not to be coming from the other side of the doors at all, but from somewhere behind her left shoulder. A hushed rumble, low and long like a storm, slowly building in intensity as it moved over the flats off of Highway 16 and continued moving closer. There was no mistake about it and, though she couldn't explain how, it sounded angry.

She heard that familiar voice faintly call out, and stepped forward to the doors. The noise behind her grew louder still and sounded as though whatever made it was near enough to take hold of the neck of her bathrobe – if that's what it really wanted to do. Though she couldn't imagine anything actually wanting to touch something as painfully uncomfortable as a wool bathrobe. She put a foot on the top steps of the cellar and heard the voice call out in its hypnotic, dulcet tones.

"Yessss…"

Isobel refused to turn around, even if she wasn't certain what made the sounds behind her. Rather than attempt to ponder the reason that dwells within a total absence of logic, she walked to the bottom of the stairs and leaned up to pull the doors closed, but not before the three small, furry, brown field mice leaped onto the arm of her robe.

The room seemed larger than it had been that afternoon, as though its earlier stretching with her movement had left a permanent deformity on the far end of it. The door she had nearly gone through was still very much intact, and now, very much open. It cast a viridian glow around the room that shone over everything in varying shades of green.

"Come," the voice said, and at once she felt the tug of the hook.

She walked toward the door and felt the writhing and gentle nibbling of the mice in her pocket, but was at once powerless to stop herself.

"Now," the voice said, and she moved silently to within a step of the door.

"Yesss…" the voice said, and before panic halted her footfalls and told her to turn back, she was sucked through the door.

EIGHT

As Isobel was unceremoniously sucked into her present surroundings, the large stone door that had appeared in the far wall of the storm cellar disappeared. Behind it, a sudden expanse of thick plants and small, green, leafy trees that bore a resemblance to the cedar shrubs lining the front yard came into view. Beyond the small cedars lay a vast and dense forest she took to be Seonagh's Woods.

"Well, shit," she sighed, and headed off in the direction of the thickest group of trees.

She walked for a few minutes, away from where the door had been, and found herself in the middle of a clearing alive with activity. There were stalls and the backs of wagons occupying every available inch of the clearing brimming with crockery and metal work, meats and cheeses, and dried fish, and loop after loop of smoked sausages thick as a baby's arm. The air hung heavy with the scent of unfamiliar spices – sharp, pungent, and exotic. The aromas wafting from cooking fires reminded her of breakfast fry ups on Sunday mornings.

The square thronged with activity and near deafening levels of sound. So many voices and clangs and bashes came from everywhere all at once. Isobel covered her ears and dropped to her knees, trying to block out the awful, confusing din.

"Suk-suk?" the vendor in front of her asked.

Isobel looked at her in stunned silence.

"Suk-suk?" the vendor repeated.

Isobel heard the voice of her mother, and could fairly feel the wide-handed wallop that always accompanied "don't stare". But she did stare. The vendor looked small, smaller than Isobel, and she wore a shabby brown woolen smock that covered her from chest nearly to ankle. Her skin looked swarthy and olive hued. Most of her shoulder length chestnut hair had been tied away from her face and slightly above the crown of her head by a thin scrap of dirty brown muslin.

The young interloper thought the vendor looked like river men she'd seen eating at the Gimbel's lunch counter. Weathered, as someone who spent a lifetime eking a living out of doors. Spending their lives moving from town to town wondering if the next place held feast or famine. Were it not for the horns, Isobel was fairly certain this could have been any one of the snake oil sellers who came through Winterbourne to sell their wares during the harvest fete every autumn.

Wait, what? Isobel thought. Horns?

Jutting out of the weathered merchant's forehead were two delicate, honey-coloured horns that didn't look out of place so much as they gave the woman a slightly more animalian appearance than she had a moment before.

"Suk-suk?" the horned woman said again. "Would you like some suk-suk? You look a little peaked."

"What are you?" Isobel blurted, and immediately regretted asking such a blunt question to a complete stranger, horned or not.

"I'm a confectioner, of course." The horned woman sighed. "Do you get your suk-suk from the butcher?"

Isobel made a small, half gurgling noise; at a complete loss for a response to give her.

"Honestly," the horned woman grumbled. "You try to offer some folks a little hospitality."

She turned her back to Isobel and moved off in the direction of the wagon. As the small woman turned, Isobel let go a shocked gasp when she saw that the woman's smock did not conceal the back of her legs as it did the front. The woman with the horns walked around on short, sturdy, very hairy *goat* legs. Isobel peered around at the other wagons and stalls, and became painfully aware they too, were peopled by half-goat things. Not a single one of them paid any more attention to her apart from trying to entice her into buying whatever they were selling. In fact, unlike her, they were so entirely unfazed by what she looked like or what she was doing there, that she could've been a talking duck before most of them would sit up and take notice.

A lone goat-like thing stepped into the middle of the square, and began plunking away on a stringed instrument resembling a hide-wrapped cigar box with a flat neck extending from one side and ending in a carving of a horned man's head. He continued strumming and, in short order, four others like himself joined in, all carrying similar instruments.

Isobel sensed the musicians were about to break into song and covered her mouth to stifle a laugh, imagining she was about to hear something akin to when her father set the speed too high on the Victrola. But what she did hear was nearly as shocking as their appearance.

The five of them stopped playing simultaneously and took a breath, audible even to Isobel who sat more than fifty feet away. If there was a lower sound that Isobel had ever heard in her life, she couldn't remember it. If there was a sound that made her feel like a key part of the world around her, the girl couldn't remember ever hearing it until that very second.

Each of the five sang a note that seemed impossibly low to be coming from something so small. At the same time, they all sang a note above the constant low drone that was almost a whistle, and danced around the backs of their throats.

"Two notes at once?" Isobel whispered. "How can anybody sing two notes at once?"

She closed her eyes and felt her mind numbing from the whistling voices over the incessant droning of the low tones.

"Yesss," the voice said. It had returned to her mind, as if summoned by the song, and resumed whispering its honey sweetened words, lulling her to follow it.

She was a little surprised to hear it again, and a little intrigued, but not enough of either to move from her spot behind the wagon.

"Come," the voice said, and the five droned on.

The song changed in its rhythm and sounded as though they sang "Mah-zoho-la" followed by shorter, one syllable words she couldn't make out. It was entrancing as it chugged along and she pushed up to one knee as if commanded to do so by the drone.

"Mah-zoho-la," they droned, and she rose from her knees altogether and assumed a full crouch behind the confectioner's wagon.

"Yesss," the voice called out to her. She stood to her full height.

"Mah-zoho-la," the five droned and Isobel felt her body move from her hiding spot behind the wagon, though she really didn't want to.

"Yesss," the voice breathed in an altogether dreamy quality. "Come child of–"

The voice cut off suddenly as if it were about to blurt out something vitally important, but prevented itself from doing so. Isobel suddenly felt a ray of clarity and turned her attention to the back of the confectioner's wagon once more. The voices grew louder, the droning more intense, and soon she walked blindly toward the market square again.

"Mah-zoho-la," the five droned louder, and Isobel's resistance faded, shrank away.

She extended both arms, closed her eyes, and moved forward in bewildered obedience.

"Yessss," the voice hissed its delighted approval and stretched out with unseen fingers to grab hold of her. Isobel's mind surrendered to the sugar-coated venom.

NINE

The form moved silently and lithely down Parker Street, darting behind what few cars were left on the main drag at six o'clock on a Sunday morning. Darting in and out of the still darkened alleyways between the buildings that dotted the route cheek-to-jowl along either side, the dark figure crept along, careful to remain in the shadows. Its movements were not random however, having made this journey several times before, but never with the gnawing urgency that drove it onward now.

The little creature heard the approach of a mother and child, and ducked into the shadows cast by the crisp, new morning sun against the side wall of Maddox's drug store.

"Did you see that, Mummy?" the small boy puzzled.

"See what, Gilbert?" the mother said, puffing loudly to move a fallen lock of bleach blonde hair out of her face.

"The little man," the boy answered. "The furry little man in the red shirt."

He froze on the spot, large brown eyes locked on the boy's gaze, mouth quaking in a terror-filled attempt to contain frightened breaths coming in short, shallow gulps. The boy pointed to him and began to speak in earnest as his mother pulled him onward.

"Yes, Gilbert," the woman sighed. "A little man in a red shirt."

Karl Draper pulled the rack of beer glasses past the front of the new dishwasher that Mrs. Butler had bought for the bar. She told him how to load the glasses into the front of the machine, told him how much time it would save washing three dozen glasses at the same time, but Karl believed no machine, no new-fangled device, would save as much time as not actually ever washing the beer glasses, just the way he hadn't been for more years than he could remember. He just set the last of the glasses on the drying rack after a cursory rinse under the wash sink hose when he heard the scraping noise at the back door.

"He's early," Karl said, glancing at the big fluorescent-ringed clock on the back wall of the bar.

The barman lifted the folding bar top, and ambled toward the staircase that led to the steel double doors. He reached for the latch to unlock the them but stopped short, remembering today was Sunday and just after six in the morning. A knock sounded, small, barely perceptible at first, and then, after a second, it came again. This time however, it was louder and with greater force. A small voice followed.

"Please," the voice said.

Karl stood at the base of the stairs, his hand still outstretched and beginning to tremble nervously, contemplating his next move. A knowing dread gnawed at him and whisper – just who was on the other side of the door? If he opened the it, his involvement in whatever the owner of the voice wanted was almost a certainty. If he did not open the door, however, and the voice and everything along with it was discovered by the people of Winterbourne – the man shuddered to think what might happen.

"Please," the voice pleaded. "Please, Karl-friend, Redheart needs your help."

Karl Draper shot his hand up to the bolt, slid it back, unlocked the door, and pulled it back in one rapid motion. As he did so, the figure on the other side fell through. Without much thought, the barman caught the collapsing form before he hit the steps, and lifted him up. Karl walked with the writhing thing to the back office, and laid him down on Mrs. Butler's worn-out fainting couch. He then wandered out to the bar, looking for the first aid kit.

When he returned to the office, the visitor paced the room, waiting for Karl to return.

"You should really be resting," Karl said.

"Redheart is strong yet," he replied with a resounding voice.

He appeared small, not much larger than a child of eight or ten, but the full, chestnut brown beard flecked with silver, dispelled any questions about his maturity. The diminutive visitor's eyes shone steel grey and full of purpose, and he emanated a confidence and determination that told all who encountered him he was not to be trifled with. They were spaced evenly between a thin, straight nose ending in a slight point above narrow lips that were a little downturned, giving the appearance of a perpetual frown.

Redheart wore clothes that were clearly much too large for him, striped flannel pyjama bottoms rolled up at the bottom at least half a dozen times, a black wool turtle-necked sweater with a crimson brocade smoking jacket over top. Topping off the entire outfit, a ridiculous floppy straw sun hat. It sat low on his head, and threatened to make his face disappear entirely beneath it if a decent gust of wind came up. The whole bizarre thing looked like the sort of disguise one would wear if it were their desire to draw immediate and constant attention to themselves.

"You don't have to wear those in here, you're safe for now," Karl said.

"The eyes of man are everywhere, I will remain in the travelling clothes," the small man replied.

"Suit yourself," Karl said.

"Redheart will suit himself, Karl-friend. Redheart will suit himself and the man-flock will tremble."

"Why are you talking like that?"

"What?" he replied. "Talking like what?"

"In that ridiculous, movie house, pidgin English?"

"Ah, right," the small man said. "I've forgotten that you lot don't expect us to be noble savages any longer and bloody well rid of it if you ask me."

"Where are you injured?"

"What makes you think I'm injured?"

"You fell when I opened the door."

"I fell because you opened the door."

"What are you doing here?" Karl quickly changing the subject.

The small man removed his floppy sun hat to reveal a delicate set of horns growing upward out of the sides of his head. He eyed the barman as he slipped out of the rest of his oversized clothing, save for a bright red waistcoat with a fine silver chain hanging from the right breast pocket. Redheart folded the oversized clothes with great reverence, and placed them gingerly inside the battered leather satchel he wore. The faun began to pace back and forth on, now uncovered, goat legs, never taking his eyes off the lantern chinned barman.

"I don't know where to begin," Redheart said.

"The beginning is traditionally the best place to start."

Redheart shot the bartender a look that said the only less appropriate thing he could have done just then, apart from making the joke he made, would have been farting in church.

The faun reached into the satchel, pulled a heavy, leather bound journal, and flipped through its age-yellowed pages. After several minutes of silent skimming. With the desired passage located, he held the book up to Karl Draper's face.

"Have you seen this before?" The little faun pushed the book toward the barman.

"The black sun?" Karl said. "Your mother told me about this. It's a fairy story meant to make young fauns behave. Eat your sprouts or Urisk will come and get you. Right?"

"Yes," Redheart said. "That's the one. Only it's not a story for the most part."

"What do you mean, for the most part?"

"The story goes like this, Urisk, the first and most powerful of our kind, came down from the mountains."

"Mountains?" Karl sputtered. "Here in Winterbourne?"

"No. Some large mountains, somewhere else. Most likely near the border."

"Border of what?

"Look, forget the mountains, will you?" Redheart sighed. "It's practically all allegorical anyway."

"Right," Karl said, feeling more than a little embarrassed.

"So, he came down form the mountain, whatever bloody mountain you would like it to be. When he did, the first men thought him a wild beast and pierced his side with their wicked spears."

"I remember always feeling bad about that part of the story."

"You should, child of the first men," Redheart smiled.

"Do go on."

"Urisk ran from the first men, into Seonagh's woods, what the fauns call Na Doireachan, where he knew the first men would not follow."

"Still won't'." Karl shuddered.

"They say that he walked for three days and three nights to reach the centre of the woods, which I've always thought was a tad on the generous side. I mean, you could make it to the middle in a day if you were travelling at a decent clip. Really, even at a leisurely pace it wouldn't take you more than a day and a half, and they say that Urisk was two and a half fauns high, so it stands to reason that he would be going faster than the average faun. I honestly don't know where the three days came from. Perhaps he got lost somewhere along the way and had to start again. Twice."

"And then?" Karl said.

"Oh… I suppose… oh, right. He made it to the heart of the woods where he met with Seonagh and they coupled, making us…"

"Yes, yes, I remember all of that. He lived for a thousand years and wrote the laws and prophecies for all fauns for years to come, and when he passed, a mighty fountain sprung forth from the earth in the very spot he fell. But what does this have to do with… anything?"

"The moon, Karl. Have you noticed the moon?"

"It does seem like we've had a full moon for an awfully long time."

"The moon has been new for four solid weeks now. As it begins to wane, rather like it's doing now, the black sun will emerge."

"So?" Karl said. "It'll be dark for a few nights until it puts itself right again."

"No. Well, yes, but it's the prophecies he left behind. Urisk wrote that he would bestow all of his strength, all of his power, on any faun willing to shed the blood of the first men under the light of the black sun."

"Um, I think I am still missing something…" Karl said slowly.

"Urisk was ready to give his full power to the first faun who was willing to murder a descendant of first men as revenge for their attack on him all those years before. Is that clear enough, or shall I draw you a diagram?"

"Clear enough. But isn't there a 'yin' to all of this?"

"A what?"

"A light to all of this dark. A balance, an opposite, a—"

"A child of nature?" the faun mused.

"Not what I was going to say, but all right."

"The child of nature is the only thing that can stop the one who has claimed the gift of Urisk," Redheart explained. "A being of absolute purity to stop something vile and profane from entering the world and causing the ruin of us all. And I have found her."

"Great!" Karl said. "Where is she? Shouldn't we be going to get her and girding up our loins?"

James Redheart let go a defeated sigh and lowered his head.

"What? Where is she, James?"

"Currently, she is being lured to the fountain at the centre of Seonagh's woods by Lucerne III, king of all fauns, where he will kill her and then make war on all the first men of Winterbourne."

TEN

Winslow rolled over in his bed, and leaned to get a cigarette from the night stand. Inching his way up to a sitting position, more or less, the priest took a long drag from the Chesterfield, and slid back down as he exhaled the smoke. His body remained comfortably in the bed but his mind had long ago woken up and gone exploring.

Old man Winterbourne made it out of there in one piece. And with a statue that's probably worth a fortune, but he still wanted to go back. He was already rich but he still wanted to go back.

"What would make a tight fisted old bastard go back into that awful place except the opportunity to get richer?"

Father Brennan got out of bed, pulled on a pair of sweatpants, and wrapped himself in a tattered woollen bathrobe, then headed into his office. If A. H. Winterbourne was anything like the priest, he would have kept some sort of record, something to keep track of everything with the slightest monetary value to it. If there was a fortune in Seonagh's Woods, then the old man would have written it down somewhere. Not necessarily an obvious place but somewhere that would remind him and enflame his covetousness all the more, every time his eyes even glimpsed the corners of it.

"Greed doth beget only greed" Father Brennan said.

Where would a man, consumed by a lust for wealth, put information that could potentially earn more wealth? Brennan pulled a fresh Chesterfield from the pack in the pocket of the bath robe and a wooden match from the other pocket. He flicked the match to life with a thumbnail and put the naked flame to the end of the cigarette. The young priest breathed the smoke in and held it, began to feel a little light headed, and then let it go slowly and deliberately while walking out of the office.

Brennan headed back to the bedroom, entirely absorbed and dragging ceaselessly on the cigarette, he rubbed his temples and flopped down on the large double bed. And then a smile scraped its way across desiccated morning lips, a bloated, gloatingly satisfied smile. Father Brennan's hand found its way inside the folds of the grey sweatpants and as it found its mark, he breathed.

"His ledger, it's in his ledger!"

He sat bolt upright, and made his way hurriedly to the rectory library.

The priest knew he'd seen old man Winterbourne's ledgers somewhere in the rectory library and as he headed in that direction, Brennan felt fairly certain that finding them would be easy enough once he actually got in there. Somehow the church had ended up with all of the Winterbourne family's belongings, but none of the vast fortune that so obviously remained after they all died. All of that money conveniently disappeared when heretofore unmentioned back taxes were levied against the estate. Funny how city hall and the courthouse both got a facelift, shortly after Parker Street received a new traffic light, and the back taxes were never spoken of again.

There were twelve, large, extravagantly bound ledgers that belonged to "The Estate of Mr. A. H. Winterbourne" and while flipping casually through them, Father Brennan could see old man Winterbourne was meticulous to a fault, and not the type of person to casually overlook something as monumental as years of missed income tax payments.

"New traffic light," Brennan sneered.

Winslow sorted through the ledgers thoroughly, page by painstaking page, starting with the very first book. But by the time he reached number four, three hours had managed to pass and he was nearly cross-eyed with the tedium of it all.

Maybe if I start from the back and work forward. He opened the last page of ledger number twelve and was met with a blank page. Twenty-six blank pages in all. Father Brennan felt a little foolish. It was starting to look like A. H. Winterbourne was just a crazy old man who went much crazier, and killed his family. But as he turned over page number twenty-four, his mood brightened.

There, written in old man Winterbourne's own elaborate hand, were the words: "The secret is in the trees." Father Brennan threw the ledger to the floor and lit a Cigarette.

"The secret is in the trees… the secret is in the trees. Of course, the secret is in the God-damned trees, it's a God-damned forest!"

The priest didn't want to go into that awful place so woefully unprepared, but it appeared now, that it was exactly what he was going to have to do. He packed a valise and prepared for disappointment as the doorbell to the rectory rang.

"What can I do for you, Tom?" Father Brennan askedthe church groundskeeper, his voice dripping with enough sickly-sweet approbation he nearly gagged as the words left his mouth.

Tom took off his cap, and began to wring it in his hands.

"It's Mrs. Kiel, she's taken another one of her spells."

"Oh, that old woman has more spells than a wizard."

"At first I thought it was like all the others, that she would come around after a while if I just let her lie there, but Father, her face. She's as grey as a badger's ass."

"Charming," Father Brennan said. "Right then, let's go and have a look at Mrs. Kiel."

She lay flat out in front of one of the flowerbeds and was cold and stiff by the time the two of them arrived. By the look on her face, it was no spell, but a full-blown heart attack that felled her.

"She's definitely as grey as a badger's ass," Father Brennan said. He bent down and begrudgingly felt her forehead. He recoiled and snapped his hand back, she felt as cold as ice.

"Um… Um… I guess we should call somebody to get her out of here, right? We can't leave her out here all day."

Tom stood still, not certain what the next course of action should be.

"Yes? You were waiting for something? Like maybe she would stop being dead and give you a hand to carry herself to the back of the church hall, perhaps?"

"Shouldn't… shouldn't you say something, father? Words and such, like the last rites or what have you?"

"Oh, for the love of… all right," Father Brennan griped. "These are the best of times and they are also the worst of times and now Mrs. Kiel is dead. Oh Lord, it sure would be swell if you could just take her into your bosom and whatnot. Amen. Now can you get her out of here before she starts stinking up the geraniums?"

Tom stood in silence, trying to act as reverend as he possibly could, knowing full well Mrs. Kiel's immortal soul had about as much chance of getting to heaven on those words as it did if it hitched a ride on the next dirigible that happened by.

"Go get the wheel barrow and get her out of here," the priest said.

"Yes father."

"Tom?" Father Brennan began.

"Father?"

"What do you know about Seonagh's woods?"

"Don't dawdle foolish child and…"

"Wait, wait," Brennan interrupted. "Is that stupid rhyme the extent of your knowledge about the comings and goings of Seonagh's woods?"

"Pretty much. The rest is just rumours, really."

"What rumours?"

"Well, there was the one about old man Winterbourne and what he brought out of there."

"He brought a statue out of there, so what?"

"No, well, yes, he brought a statue out, that much is true, but he also brought out the wrath of whatever was in there."

"What?"

"Old man Winterbourne went in there when he was in his forties. When he came out of there after two days, it was as a man in his seventies. He went on and on about the devil living in those woods and there being more wealth than any man could spend and how it rightly belonged to him. Three weeks later he burned himself, his family, and that palace of a house to cinders."

"After we get rid of the dear departed Mrs. Kiel, I want you to go into the rectory and get the bag that's in my bedroom."

"What are you planning to do, Father?"

"I am not planning anything. We're going into Seonagh's woods and get whatever is in there out."

"Father, no!"

"Relax," Father Brennan said. "If the Devil really lives in there, who better to get us through it than a priest?"

ELEVEN

Isobel drifted along with the music, arms drawn out and body gliding mindlessly forward. She moved as though pulled by delicate, silken strands not knowing, or caring, if a puppeteer or spider waited at the end of them. As the music changed to a livelier, less-sombre sounding tune, she found herself caught up in the middle of a thronging, rollicking crowd of goat things. The crowd became a singular, pulsing entity, swaying and thronging in time with the joyful noise the five singers were now making, and they were taking the girl along for the ride.

The little blonde girl suddenly felt alive like she never had before, and threw back her head to let the laughter bubble out of her. She thought about her mother, frowning a million miles from here and danced harder, and laughed louder. After all, what was the point of having fun if you couldn't stick your finger in the eye of the people who wanted you to have the least amount of it?

The music stopped abruptly and a hush fell over the crowd, though Isobel remained exuberantly unaware and continued to dance alone with all the grace of a penguin suffering from an inner ear condition. She became horribly aware, somewhere in her rhythmic flailing, that the music had stopped and she had not. Isobel stopped dancing, felt hundreds of eyes upon her, and stood helpless and alone amid the pointing and terrible derisive laughter.

She sighed. "Even in an enchanted bloody forest, I can't catch a God-damned break."

Isobel put both hands in her pockets, lowered her head, and waited for the awful laughter to stop.

"SILENCE!" a gigantic voice said and the laughter did stop, as though it had run into a wall.

A thick muscular faun, easily a whole head taller than the others in the crowd, with dark skin and broad, strong, black horns spiralling from his temples, stepped into the square followed by two slightly shorter but no less muscular fauns. He motioned for the two to stand firm and walked to the girl with a fast and angry stride. From his gait and the speed with which he crossed the square, Isobel got the impression his being made to talk to a silly little human child was an insult beyond measure to someone of his standing.

"Do you speak?" the thick faun barked at Isobel.

The Schneider girl had always believed that at some point in her life, she would cross paths with something, some being, that was different enough to make her sit up and take note. As a matter of record, the very last thing she figured such a fantastical being, such as the one she currently conversed with, would ask her was whether or not she had the power to form words.

"What?" Isobel fumbled, taken completely off guard by the faun's question.

"Oh dearie, dearie me," the faun said. "This is going to be difficult, isn't it?"

"Isn't it?" the two thugs on the outside of the square clucked.

The larger faun shot them a look that would wither flowers and the two of them snapped to attention, understanding from that point forward, goonery of any sort would be dealt with swiftly and terribly.

"Do – you - speak?" the faun shouted at her.

"I'm not deaf."

"Ah well, let's get on with it then, shall we? No need to keep everyone longer than needed, yes?"

"Of course," Isobel said hopefully. "I suppose we should introduce ourselves, shouldn't we?"

"Ye gawds," the faun moaned. "If you think it's absolutely necessary."

"Wouldn't you think it is?"

"Oh, you humans and your need to name everything. That is a tree and that is a river and that is a platypus, great bloody name on that one by the way, very well. I am Maurice Chevalier Dreadhorn. Sergeant at arms and high protector to his supreme majesty Lucerne III king of all fauns. And you are?"

"Umm… well… I am Isobel Schneider, aged fourteen."

"Fascinating," Dreadhorn said.

"Well I am only fourteen," Isobel answered.

"But of course you are, dear."

"Have you come to tell me why I am here?"

"Ah!" Dreadhorn beamed in buoyant, mocking tones. "Perhaps not so human after all?"

Isobel had never considered one of her strongest suits to be recognizing sarcasm in any form, and so wasn't certain if his statement was meant as a compliment or mockery, and remained silent for fear of offering him insult in either case.

He unrolled a long, tanned piece of parchment. "I am here as an emissary of his majesty to not only welcome you to the hallowed oaks and ferns of Na Doireachan, but also to tell you that your coming here is not by chance…"

"Of course it isn't," Isobel interrupted.

"Hadn't finished," Dreadhorn persisted.

"I'm sorry?"

"No, no, do go on. I'm certain that whatever it was you were about to say was almost certainly superior, and in every way more important than the decree of the king of all fauns."

"I followed a voice here," Isobel said quietly. "Through a door in the back of my storm cellar."

"How's that?" Dreadhorn said smugly. "Come again? Didn't quite catch that last bit."

"I said I followed a voice and came here through a door in the back of my storm cellar, so it couldn't be by chance."

"A voice! And whose voice was it?" Dreadhorn asked.

"Oh," mused Isobel. "I hadn't given it much thought."

"Come, come, it's surely not that difficult." Dreadhorn declared.

"Was it your voice I followed?"

Dreadhorn threw the scroll to the ground and it snapped back into a roll like a loose window blind. "Do you see the horns?" Dreadhorn demanded.

"What?"

"Horns girl. Do you see the pronounced horns curling outward from my head?"

"Well, yes," she said, not certain where the faun's questions were leading.

"You notice then, the complete and total lack of a crown or other such regal paraphernalia?"

"Yes," Isobel admitted, feeling stupid for having been sucked into his word games again.

"So then, I haven't the foggiest. Not an iota of an idea, not the minisculest morsel of the tiniest flicker of cerebellar activity as to what his majesty has in mind for you this morning."

"Oh. All right."

He went on, "And therefore I would have no business using my voice or any other to bring you here, or anywhere else, without his majesty's express wishes to do so."

"Gotcha," Isobel said.

"May I finish now?"

"What?"

"I had been reading from this parchment and would like to finish just that. If that is entirely alright with you," Dreadhorn spat.

"Oh, of course," Isobel answered.

"Nothing else pressing, no matters of great importance you feel you need to share just now?"

"No. Not a thing," the girl answered.

"Very well. I am here as an emissary of his majesty to not only welcome you to the hallowed oaks and ferns of Na Doireachan, but also to tell you that your coming here is not by chance. Long has your coming been foretold to us and now the ancient tales have become the modern times and soon they will be the glorious history of our two proud peoples and the times of the great kings of Sacred Woods will come again."

"Oh?" Isobel wondered aloud.

"Indeed. If you wouldn't entirely mind waiting here, I'm certain someone will be along shortly to...attend to you."

"Oh...ah...alright. And thank you," Isobel said and bowed low to the faun.

"I live to serve," Dreadhorn sneered, doing little containing the annoyance in his voice.

He snapped his fingers as he walked and the two muscular fauns fell in line behind him. The three of them disappeared behind a large building at the western-most edge of the square, leaving Isobel standing there, feeling confused and vulnerable. From the front of the building emerged two small fauns carrying large brass horns much larger than themselves. And as they lifted them to their lips, they were forced to steady the instruments across the railings that surrounded the back of the enormous dwelling.

The trumpeters sounded a flat, confusing tune that left Isobel and the remaining assembled fauns bewildered as to what they were actually announcing. When a faun, resplendent in silks and finery, emerged from the large building, the crowd of fauns applauded wildly and cheered as he walked about on the platform behind the dwelling.

The regal satyr made his way over to Isobel and stopped in front of her, stripping himself of his extravagant looking vestments and bowed low before the girl.

"My dear, I have been waiting for you for longer than you could possibly know."

"You have?"

"Yesssss," Lucerne III hissed. "And in time you will save every living faun in this forest."

TWELVE

Redheart tossed back the contents of his glass in one, long, steady swallow, and moved to stand up from the bar stool, swaying and tipping to one side as his balance began to leave him. A chuckle left his lips as he over adjusted the movement to right himself and tipped in the opposite direction.

"Wait," Karl said. "Shouldn't we be doing something?"

"We are doing something. We're getting drunk and feeling sorry for ourselves."

"I thought something a touch more rescue-ish."

"You don't think I thought of that?" Redheart slurred. "Shomething Reshcue-ish?"

"And?"

"And what?"

"And what did you come up with?" Karl enunciated every syllable as he spoke.

"Well, as near as I can remember, a door needs to open for someone to get in."

"Didn't you leave by a door? Couldn't we just find that one and go back in it?"

"I didn't leave, I was unceremoniously, bloody thrown out!" he fumed, and began to disconnectedly refill his glass, putting as much liquid on the counter of the bar as he managed to get in the bottom of the glass.

He looked up and slightly left, and held his attention in the general direction of the mirror at the back of the bar.

"What are you looking at?" Karl inquired.

"Na Doireachan," Redheart said, raising his glass in a boozy, heartfelt toast. "Seonagh's woods, my glorious homeland."

"Which is currently over your right shoulder," Karl said.

"Oh, you humans and your bloody details," Redheart said. "The forest is behind your right shoulder, always mind your P's and Q's, those aren't your trousers. Honestly."

Karl stared at the rambling drunken faun for a time, wanting to say something to introduce a handful of sense into his liquored-up diatribe but thought better of it and quickly changed the subject.

"You were saying about doors?"

"Ah, right. Na Doireachan is protected by charms and whatnot, magical gates and that sort of falderal. Never had much use for it myself, but I understand their necessity."

"Really," Karl asked, slightly dumbfounded. "Wasn't your father... and aren't you–"

"Really," Redheart blurted. "It's the deep, dark woods and it is peopled, almost entirely, by things that you lot think are evil incarnate. How do you think it would go if somebody wandered in and found out what was really in there?"

"I never thought of it that way."

"The Devil walks along Grey Hollow Road," Redheart spat. "And if you found out the Devil was harmless or had a wife and child, what would you brutes do then?"

The faun began to pace the room, drunkenly and muttering loudly to himself. The barman feared that, if left like this too long, the little faun might never recompose himself and tell him what all of this was about.

"And the doors?" Karl said attempting to steer the conversation back to the neighbourhood of the point.

"Right," the faun said, calming slightly. "Because of the charms around it, doors must be opened in order to enter the sacred grove. That is how the child of nature got in there, a door was opened to her somewhere."

"And how does one open a door?"

"There's the rub. Only the king of all fauns has the power and the authority to open doors as he sees fit," Redheart said.

"Ah. I guess we can't ask him to just open another one?"

"He's not taking my calls just now."

Karl sat beside the faun at the bar and poured a stiff shot of top-shelf whisky. Draining it, delicately into his gullet and holding it upside down for an inordinate amount of time, making certain not to waste a single drop of the golden drink. And when he was satisfied he had emptied the tumbler wholly and completely, he up ended it, and slammed it emphatically onto the counter top. The impact echoed through the empty bar like a shotgun blast and sent thousands of tiny shards across the Formica like cockroaches scattering in the cold fluorescent glare of the kitchen light.

"So, we're screwed?" Karl said, his voice barely audible beneath the weight of defeasance.

"Blued and tattooed." And after a moment or two of uncomfortable silence, James Redheart offered, "There is one other who opens doors, but she is of no use."

"Who? If there is someone else, we need to find her and get her to open a door, right?"

"The *old one* can open doors."

"She's a legend though."

"It's been so long since anyone has seen her, you might think that. She was always a bit... off as I understand, but that kind of power never comes without a certain amount of oddity."

"Where did she disappear?"

James Redheart eyed his friend the barman with a look that summed up the fundamental reasons why humans always seemed to find themselves at loggerheads with one another. At any given point, when a human being finds himself in a position to add something profound to a weighted conversation, he will almost certainly say the first, and thereby stupidest, thing that springs from the uppermost reaches of his brain and travels to his mouth. Along with wondering if a blue streak across the middle of a canned ham is still all right to eat.

"If we knew where she disappeared to, Karl, we could have just gone back to that spot and looked." Redheart sighed.

"No," Karl barked, sounding more than a little defensive. "I meant, if you were going to look for her, where would you start?"

"She was last seen looking for winter things near the western tip."

"And that is where, exactly?"

"The western tip of Seonagh's woods looks out onto the edge of the Winterbourne estate."

Karl sat very still, his attention moving between the ceiling and the tops of his shoes as though an answer might miraculously appear in the void between the two at any moment. Working things out was never his strongest suit. In fact, if Karl Draper had a strong suit, it would have been anything that avoided the word work in any of its applications. A smile of realization eased its way across his face and faded into discouraged ignorance again as a mighty train of thought careened off the side of a mountain inside his head. He sighed and felt the weight of hopelessness park itself squarely on his shoulders when a tiny steam engine began chugging its way back up the mountain.

Karl's excited brain belched out a question.

"What was she wearing?"

"Have you taken complete leave of your senses?"

"I mean, would she have been dressed like you were?" Karl sputtered excitedly.

"She would have been wearing travelling clothes, yes. But I don't see what–"

"And you said she acted a bit… odd?"

"Well yes. But I still don't–"

"I know where she is," Karl crowed.

THIRTEEN

Isobel Schneider took a meagre sip from the ornate silver goblet the small faun had brought to her on a gleaming silver platter. The dark and bitter liquid had a pungent aroma like roof pitch. She looked about at her surroundings and found she was in a large room with all manner of food laid out on a long, thick-legged, carved, oak table. From thick, fat buns of good course bread, and meats of every description; joints of beef and pork and roast chickens by the dozen and exotic fruits that she had only seen in the window of Murray's grocery store. She was starving and the food had bewitched her senses absolutely, though she didn't dare touch it until someone came along and told her it was all right.

There had been no sign of the king since he met her in the square and suggested she come take some refreshment before they discussed the favour he would ask of her.

"Very powerful," she whispered.

Only she didn't feel powerful, but exactly like a frightened, slightly odd, young girl who, as always, was caught up in something very much over her head. Isobel wished her father had been there. In the beginning, Ezra would give her hell for doing something so foolish again. But, when it came right down to it, there'd be a smile and a warm, long hug and a father would tell his daughter how proud he was of her for not being afraid to give life a kick in the guts.

Still, Isobel thought, it would have been nice not to be alone right now.

The nervous blonde girl felt a squirm inside the right pocket of the scratchy, bathrobe and realized she wasn't alone after all.

"You slept through everything up 'til now?"

Three twitching noses followed by three sets of coal black eyes emerged from the tartan wool pocket, squeaking their ignorance.

"Well I thought it was quite exciting," she said. "The king has a favour to ask of me."

The three of them looked at her as though she had suggested there was a great horned owl in one of her other pockets and it was now their duty as the new tenants, to ask it to leave.

"What?"

They squeaked a heated reply as they walked down the length of her arm and onto the table, staring intently at the feast.

"Trust him just enough to stuff our faces, do we?"

An embarrassed series of squeaks followed.

"Quickly then," she relented. "And then right back into the pocket."

The mice dashed toward the gigantic meal and crammed as much into their faces as mousely possible.

"Besides," she said. "Why would a king ask me a favour if he only meant to do me harm? Seems very un-kingly."

She heard the bolt toggle on the door and it suddenly dawned on her that she had been locked into the great hall. Isobel tweeted a quick and quiet whistle, and the three mice hurriedly replaced themselves in her pocket.

The door swung open, and in walked Dreadhorn followed by his two, ever present, goons. The larger faun scanned the room and proceeded to make his way over to her.

"Young miss?"

"Isobel, please."

"Very well. Isobel?"

"Yes Maurice," Isobel said with a smirk. The idea of someone so completely fierce and singular of purpose being called Maurice was too amusing to her to go unnoticed.

"Dreadhorn, if you please," Dreadhorn said dryly. "And it's sergeant Dreadhorn."

"Sergeant Dreadhorn."

"Yes…" the faun sputtered. "His majesty will be arriving shortly to ask a favour of you."

"Yes?"

"Yes," he replied.

"No. I meant yes as in yes, do go on."

"I know what you meant child," the faun retorted indignantly. "You don't get to be sergeant at arms just because the uniform fits, you know."

Isobel looked him over and opened her mouth to speak.

"Figure of speech," Dreadhorn said, cutting her off. "Now, his majesty will be arriving shortly and you may not speak to him until spoken to, clear?"

"Clear. But wait, I spoke to him in the square and we–"

"*Clear?*" Dreadhorn reiterated with a healthy dose of emphasis on the word.

"Clear."

"King, mind you," Dreadhorn said, raising a finger to admonish her. "Can do as he pleases, yes?"

"Of course."

"Very well. Now that we have that cleared up we may begin."

"Begin?"

"Feasting, of course."

"Feasting!" the two goons snickered, who had remained painfully silent.

"His majesty bids you eat what you like. Though"–he leaned in and spoke to her barely above a whisper–"I would prefer it if you would allow these two to dine before you. Not a pretty sight the two of them on the nosh, and it wouldn't do well to get between them and the viands if you catch my meaning?" He tapped the side of his nose knowingly.

Isobel nodded nervously. "Yes. They look as though they are starving."

The two goons looked at Isobel with gratitude as avaricious grins spread across one face and then the other. Dreadhorn snapped his fingers again and the two fauns leaped on the banquet with rattle-boned abandon. It was less like two fauns eating a feast and more like a blur of hands moving to mouths and food occasionally entering the latter.

It ended nearly as quickly as it begun; the two thick fauns pushed themselves away from the table, and resumed their positions, several healthy paces behind the larger Dreadhorn. The three fauns stood in silence, broken only by intermittent belches and hiccups as Isobel pondered the few scraps that hadn't been entirely picked clean. She managed to fill a modest plate with an even more modest piece of foul. Calling it chicken would have been far from accurate. To say it tasted like chicken was as close to identifying it as Isobel was willing to go. She feared knowing the truth would have been much less palatable. Her eyes pored over what remained of the feast and found a few crusts of good, brown bread and some bits of cheese that were hard and just pungent enough to be appealing.

Isobel ate her fill, which was nearly all of it, and pushed the plate away. She could feel the three mice squirming hungrily in her pocket and managed to sneak a decent sized crumb of the bread for them.

"All finished, then?" Dreadhorn queried.

"All <burp> finished <burp> <belch>, <hic> then?" the goons parroted.

"I think so," Isobel said, wiping her mouth. "Yes."

"I'll just pop out and fetch his majesty then, shall I?" Dreadhorn suggested, the sarcasm dripping from every word he spoke.

Dreadhorn snapped his fingers and the goons fell in line behind him, moving considerably slower now than they had on their way in. Isobel moved quickly as the fauns left and snatched up two more crusts of brown bread and stuck them into her pocket. After a time, she heard the bolt slide and again, the door arced slowly open. This time, however, the three muscular fauns were absent, and without much pomp and nearly a total lack of pageantry, in strolled Lucerne III, king of all fauns, who looked as though he hadn't a care in the world. Which, as a matter of record, he didn't. What should a king care about apart from still being a king in the morning after he had gone to bed?

The king stood at an average height for a faun, which put him at eye level with Isobel, and those eyes were emerald green and full of strength and resolve, though there was also a tiredness around them that Isobel thought might be a recent development. He pulled a chair from the table and placed it beside Isobel, looking more like a friend come over for a gab and a cup of warm cocoa, rather than the undisputed ruler of an entire race of beings.

Lucerne finally spoke, "Do you know what a king is?"

"What?" Isobel blurted defensively. "I'm not completely stupid, you know. We have got kings in places, where I come from."

The king of all fauns threw his head back and laughed loudly, and a wave of relief washed over both of them and melted away any tension that remained. Soon Isobel laughed just as heartily as he, though she wasn't entirely certain what was funny.

"The question was meant rhetorically."

"Oh," Isobel said. She was getting the gist of what he meant, though she wasn't certain she had ever heard the word rhetorically before. The elated, young girl reckoned it was likely a word in the language of fauns that couldn't be translated into English and felt honoured that he regarded her as clever enough to use his own language in front of her.

"A king is a keeper of secrets. Secrets of all kinds, and it is the duty of a king to decide what to do with those secrets. Perhaps they will help his people or do them great harm. Often they seem the same and a king must know the difference."

"Okay," she said, not really having the slightest idea what he was driving at.

"Isobel, my people are dying," he said with a solemnness and sincerity in his eyes that nearly brought her to tears.

"What?" she gasped.

"Yes." He lowered his head. "Our water source has been poisoned. And what little we have left will soon disappear."

"What can I do?" she said, feeling slightly inadequate.

Lucerne III smiled at her, and those green eyes glowed with the warmth of a father about to ask his child to go to the corner store for a loaf of bread and a bottle of milk.

"So selfless," he said and took her hand in his.

A trap clicked silently and ominously open, and though Isobel had no idea it was right in front of her, she would end up just as dead if she kept on this way.

"And so powerful." Lucerne breathed. "I can feel the strength in these hands."

She moved to pull her hand away in embarrassed discomfort but he held it all the tighter.

"A king must always know when to help his people," he said.

She nodded her head, never taking her eyes off of his.

"He must also know when it is time to call for help, to save his people."

"Oh," she whispered. "I don't know if I can do anything."

"Of course you can, my child. It is why I brought you here. You are the only one who can do it."

"What? What do you want me to do?"

A viperous smile slithered across his mouth and a crust of good, brown bread baited the trap.

"There is a deep pool in the middle of Seonagh's woods," the king began.

"A gigantic pool by our standards, and at the centre, there springs a natural fountain."

"Yes?"

"At the bottom of this pool, near where the fountain springs, many green plants with bright red tips grow. One of these will purify our waters for many years to come."

"Why don't you get Dreadhorn or one of his soldiers to go and get it?"

The king of all fauns gave a small, uncomfortable laugh. "Fauns cannot swim."

She sat silently for a time, trying to take in all the information he'd dropped on her lap. In less than a full day, Isobel had gone from wilful, chore avoiding girl to the saviour of the goat people of Seonagh's woods. It scarcely seemed real to her, and she lay in the midst of it. The weight of it all on her shoulders was palpable and the young girl turned away from him to escape the pleading in those emerald eyes.

Isobel saw a group of young fauns playing on the thick, lush grass outside the great hall. She stuck her face out of the opened window and felt the cool air of the forest as the young fauns laughed and rolled on the lawn and had no idea their days were numbered.

"They will all die if the water is not purified," he said.

One of the young fauns caught her eye and smiled up at her. She felt the tear trickle down her cheek and turned back to him.

"Okay, I'll do it," she said, and the jaws of the trap closed on her.

FOURTEEN

Father Brennan entered the front gates of Winterbourne Cemetery just after one o'clock. Tom stopped dead just inside the entrance.

"Problems?"

"This is the end of Grey Hollow Road, you know, like in the poem?" Tom said.

"And you're waiting for the Boogey Man to come out and get us, are you?"

"The Devil," Tom corrected. "A lot of folk here about believe he really walks out here on certain nights."

"And what do you believe, Tom?"

"I believe that I would have been a damn site happier about all of this if I had taken a drink or two before we came out here."

The two carried on silently for a time until they came to the Winterbourne crypt. Father Brennan reached out his hand and gently rubbed the bronze relief of old man Winterbourne's face.

"Father?"

"Tom?"

"What are we doing out here, really?"

"What are you afraid of Tom? Are you really worried the Devil is going to come up from hell and steal your immortal soul away from you and leave you out here to die on Grey Hollow Road?"

Brennan pulled at the iron rings on the doors of the mausoleum and, to his surprise, they opened with only a bit of effort. He dug around in his bag, positive a flashlight had been thrown in it. The father hastily took the box of matches from his pocket, after coming up from the bag empty handed, and struck one against the wall of the tomb. Various sized candles in sconces sat along the walls and he grabbed the longest one he could find.

"Come on," Brennan said.

With great reluctance, Tom moved into the tomb alongside the priest.

"I'll just bet that old man Winterbourne managed to take some of his money with him," Father Brennan said.

"What are you suggesting, Father Brennan?"

"What I'm suggesting, Tom, is that there is likely a small fortune inside this big marble box and nobody in here needs it anymore."

Tom walked along cautiously in the glow of the candle light. The mausoleum smelled of centuries-old must and was unexpectedly torrid. Even with the seasons gearing up for winter, the air was close and the temperature made it near to stifling inside. They walked down a short corridor and came to a set of stairs. Father Brennan held the candle out and could see from the shine coming from them that they too were made of marble.

"Nice," he breathed.

The two of them descended the four stairs and came into the room that housed the caskets of the Winterbourne family. One adult sized stone coffin, not particularly ornate, with the name plate of Mrs. Winterbourne, and two smaller plain-stone coffins, belonging to the two daughters. To the right of them lay old man Winterbourne's sarcophagus, huge in comparison to the other three. It loomed in front of the two men, a Peruvian marble monstrosity, nearly all white but for thick, creamy, green veins that sprung up randomly through it. In the candle light the fittings appeared to be brass, but Father Brennan soon realized that, with the length of time they'd been down here and the complete lack of tarnish on them, that they could only be made of gold.

The priest made a half-hearted attempt to get one of the fittings off, realizing someone who could afford such a monument to his wealth would have also paid to make sure it stayed intact. He made a silent vow to come back in here with a crow bar or tow rope and the intent to fill his pockets. Brennan moved around the room with the candle far out in front of him and took as many of the objects that glinted in the light as he could carry.

"Don't be shy Tom, they won't mind."

Tom stood dumbfounded. He had never known another priest, or another person, like Father Winslow Brennan – a priest who he had absolutely certainty was going to hell. Tom was also fairly certain if he joined in with the grave robbery he watched, he would be alongside the priest during his fiery demise.

"I've never really gone in for… antiques," Tom replied.

"Suit yourself."

Tom stood silently, squinting at the darkness while trying to make out what stood almost within arm's reach. He looked to his left and saw a small marble table with a heavy looking, silver candelabra on top of it full of unlit tapers. Taking a pipe lighter from his waistcoat pocket, the older man walked along and lit them one by one, bringing a sudden bright illumination to the darkened crypt.

With the room now noticeably brighter, Tom could clearly see what stood in front of him, and the silver candelabra nearly crashed to the floor as he laid eyes on what he couldn't make out before. The Devil did walk along Grey Hollow road, or at least inhabited the tomb in the middle of it.

"Father Brennan," Tom called out nervously. "You might want to come and look at this."

Father Brennan could see by the additional light the place looked much larger than he had initially thought. The room expanded before him as he moved forward – cavernous and covered in marble from floor to ceiling. In Brennan's best guess, you could fit at least two cars end to end, and three side by side.

He followed the light source to where Tom stood and fell to his knees, basking in the glow of the candle light reflecting off the surface of it.

"My God!" Brennan cried.

"Father!" Tom shouted.

A statue, roughly the size of an adult, though it stood on a podium making it taller than either of them. The silver arms held aloft with fingers out stretched and its head thrown back looking skyward. There were massive, stag-like horns stretching upward from the crown of the head and the expression on its full bearded face looked rapturous, but could just as easily be an expression of quiet malevolence. The figure stood naked from the waist up and below lay the furry, hoofed feet of a goat. From all appearances the entire thing, including the base, was solid silver. Beyond the silver likeness lay a small iron ladder leading down to a narrow, carved-stone entryway.

Father Winslow Brennan stretched out his hand to touch the silver effigy, and Tom quickly slapped his hand away.

"Father, you are a man of God!"

"And?" Brennan questioned, slightly confused by what the older man meant.

"Well Father, it's just that you shouldn't…"

"Tom, what do you think the Devil looks like?"

Tom stared at the ground and felt a little like a school boy who had just been asked to read poetry aloud in front of the class.

Tom didn't say anything so much as he gestured in the general direction of the statue.

"The Devil lives in the hearts of all men, Tom. You and me and everyone who was ever squeezed out into this sick, miserable, God-damned charade we call life," Brennan spat. "There is a shadow in the world, a slow creeping evil that will blanket us all in despair. It is human nature. We are creatures of habit and we wallow in our own filth like so many pigs before the slaughter. We turn a blind eye to our neighbour's plight and watch from our kitchen windows as poverty and starvation slowly bloats their bellies. The best you can ever hope for, is to get what you can and get as far away from everyone before they jam a knife between your ribs."

"I don't understand, Father."

"I am beyond reproach, un-punishable because of a black shirt and a collar. Evil is pre-packaged and ready to roll off the lot. The devil doesn't have cloven hoofs and a pointy tail, Tom. He looks like just like Uncle Sam."

FIFTEEN

Redheart and Karl knelt in the long grass that grew just beyond the back property of the Winterbourne Asylum and bordered Seonagh's Woods.

"You want me to do what?" Redheart gawped.

"Look, Just put your other clothes on and do as I say."

"This is never going to work," Redheart moaned.

The back property of the Asylum spread over a four-and-a-half acre sprawl of lush Kentucky blue grass, edged on either side by a single row of pin-straight white ash trees. The timber was perfectly aligned both vertically and horizontally. Karl laughed to himself. He'd heard Old Man Winterbourne was such a stickler about the smallest details on his estate that the trees were likely aligned on the bias as well.

In its salad days, the estate grounds had been covered in an abundant, well-manicured lawn, pock-marked by reflecting pools and deep, tranquil looking fish ponds. Once colourful wildflower gardens and granite lined paths cut through the flower beds and seemed to stretch beyond the horizon, but when the asylum took permanent residence, it became clear there were barely enough staff to keep the grass cut, never mind trying to stop the inmates from bathing and fouling in the reflecting pools and eating the fat goldfish. In the end, they resorted to filling them in with concrete which, if not as aesthetically pleasing, was considerably easier to hose out.

And if that weren't enough to remove all traces of its former majesty, the entire yard had been wrapped in an eight-foot-high, chain link fence with a guard house to the right of the only gate.

"Act mad," Karl said to Redheart as they walked slowly toward the guard house.

"You dirty son of a…" Redheart growled.

"No, no," Karl snapped out of the side of his mouth. "Mad like crazy. This is a mad house."

"Oh, right."

They were within earshot of the little wooden shack the guard sat in when Redheart broke away from Karl and ran straight for the door.

"Bongiorno Princepesa!" he squealed gleefully at the blonde-haired man in the booth and skipped away.

"What the hell?" the man said.

"Buono Natale!" Redheart shouted while bounding by.

The guard stuck his head out the window of the guard house and saw the moon face of Karl Draper, uncomfortably close and smiling back at him.

"Hiya Dave."

"Jesus!" Dave shouted. "I about gave up the ghost!"

"Sorry," Karl said.

"What's this?"

"My sister's kid. She caught him naked in the chicken house again and he threatened her with one of the birds when she tried to make him come out."

"What, what?" Dave gasped. "What do you mean he threatened her with one of the birds?"

He picked up one of the chickens, good laying hen if I remember right, grabbed the damn thing by the feet and started swinging it around at her. Kept saying he was going to pummel her, pummel her with a pullet. Feathers and chicken shit everywhere."

"Wow," Dave breathed.

"She told me to come and get him and to bring my shotgun."

"Enzo Mannacote!" Redheart bounded by again and sprang off in the direction of the big house.

"I finally convinced him to put some clothes on and get in the car, told him we were going for gelato."

Dave feigned listening as Karl related the rest of the story and pretended as though it were the craziest thing he'd ever heard. Sadly, it wasn't even the craziest thing the guard had heard today.

"Okay," Dave said. "Do you want to check him in officially or just sort of slip him in?"

"I'm sorry?" Karl asked. "Slip him in?"

"Strictly speaking not on the up and up but doing it by the books is a hellacious amount of paperwork for all of us. He's nutty enough, nobody will notice another one.

Karl hesitated. "Okay, so should I just…"

"How much money have you got?"

"Oh, there's that other shoe," Karl said. "I've got fifty bucks and Nutsy Fagin has a pocket full of the freshest chicken feathers you've ever seen."

"Not a lot, is it?" Dave smiled.

"I'm guessing it never is."

"Tell you what, you give me the fifty and the next time I find myself in Butler's with some of the boys you might just open a few of the top shelf bottles and look the other way."

Karl stared at the young guard for a time that felt too long, speechless and on the verge of telling him where exactly about his person he could store the fifty and all of the top shelf bottles too. He didn't like blackmail in principle, it was dirty business forcing people to do as you pleased for no other reason than you happened to have them over a barrel.

Karl realized, just before letting the fist he had tightly balled up fly, that his current travelling companion was a horned man with the legs of a goat who currently pranced about the grounds of the insane asylum they were attempting to break into to find a horned woman – also, with the legs of a goat and just as likely to be wearing striped pyjama bottoms. He relaxed his fist and reached for his wallet.

"Just give me a heads up before you and the boys are coming," he said, and handed over the fifty.

Dave scribbled briefly on a small piece of official Winterbourne Asylum letter head, folded, and handed it to Karl.

"Give this to the door guard and he'll take it from there."

"Thanks, Dave."

"Happy to help." He smirked and snapped the bills back and forth between his hands before stuffing them in his pocket.

Karl left the guard house and saw Redheart waiting for him patiently just outside the door. The little faun begun to walk toward the house when he stopped suddenly and gazed upward. The sun and the moon ceased their slow motion Danse Macabre and had begun to move languidly toward one another.

"It's begun," Redheart said.

"What has?"

"The black sun is coming. Soon the king will spill the blood of the first men into the fountain in Seonagh's woods."

"And then he will…" Karl stuttered, forgetting exactly what the faun had told him through the fog of liquor.

"And then he will gain more power than any faun has ever had, and start a war that will wipe out all human life in Winterbourne."

"Oh. Oh, right."

The two of them headed silently toward the large wooden door that led into the asylum.

"For the record"–Karl turned to Redheart–"you think Italian is the language of crazy?"

"I was willing to bet he didn't speak it," the faun answered.

"But Italian? You couldn't manage a few choice words in your own sacred and horrendously, confusing mother tongue?"

"Not nearly as bouncy as Italian."

"You might have warned me."

"Worked, didn't it?"

They walked up to the big door and Karl nervously handed the note to the guard. He examined it and turned his attention immediately back to Terry and her desperate adventures with and without her pirates, which blared happily away on the wood paneled Philco. The guard groped for the large black button with a finger, pushed down on it, and triggered the long, low buzz of the security door unlocking, and with no more effort than putting one foot after the other, Redheart and Karl were within the walls of Winterbourne asylum.

SIXTEEN

"Are you quite able to carry this?" Dreadhorn patronised, handing a rucksack to Isobel. "It's quite heavy."

It wasn't any heavier than her school books all bound together, or even the wash basket she carried when she hung out the washing to dry.

"It's fine."

Isobel could feel the muscular faun staring at her and she suddenly felt very self-conscious, as if he silently criticized every inch of her.

"Do all young humans dress like this?" he asked after a time.

"Like what?" She felt the need to pull the collar of her robe tightly up around her neck.

"In those robes of Scotch plaid and tall rubber shoes? I remember humans dressing very differently the last time I ventured beyond the verge."

"It was late, these aren't my clothes."

"Whose clothes are they?" the faun asked.

"Look, it was very late and I got out of bed to follow a voice into my storm cellar," she said, doing little to disguise the frustration rising in her voice.

"Do you hear a lot of voices from underground?" he prodded.

"I should think that would be something you'd be familiar with," she shot back.

The larger faun looked at her and a generous smile played across his lips.

"What are you doing here?" she asked him.

"His majesty has suggested that I accompany you on your journey to keep you safe," Dreadhorn said.

Isobel threw a look that said she might have been born during the day, but it wasn't yesterday.

"You mean you're tagging along to make sure that I don't chicken out and try to run home."

"Such a clever girl," he said lowly. "Perhaps too clever for your own good."

"Maybe just clever enough for my own good," she fired back without missing a beat.

Isobel slung the pack on her back and stood, feeling the full weight of it for the first time and thought she might have underestimated its weight. Still, she felt capable of carrying it. Dreadhorn tossed a small cloth-wrapped parcel at her.

"Eat, it's a long trip and you might just as well get used to this. It's all we'll have until we get back."

She opened the bag and saw it contained several long, thick, strips of some kind of dried meat. Though it was mostly grey and entirely unappealing. She took a bite, or as close to a bite as clamping her teeth down and moving her arm forcefully back and forth until a mouth sized chunk broke off. Chewing it was less enjoyable and it spread a flavour darker than its colour in her mouth.

"Well?" Dreadhorn asked.

"Would you be offended if I told you it tasted like a smoked rat?"

"No," he replied. "I would be amazed that you could identify the flavour after a single bite."

Isobel felt a gag rising in her throat but forced the dried meat back down for fear of losing whatever respect she gained by eating it so readily. She swallowed the rest of it down and gave him a look of confused satisfaction.

"When do we leave?" she said, smiling.

"Well now-ish. If you like. We'll walk for a full day and make camp tonight. From there we should reach the fountain by mid-day if we leave at first light."

"Oh?" Isobel said sounding a little shocked.

"Yes?" Dreadhorn asked.

"The forest doesn't look that big from the outside."

"Oh my," the thick faun said. "Losing our nerve already, are we? And not even having gotten our feet wet yet?"

"No," Isobel said defiantly. "You lead the way and I'll get the plant."

"You'll get the plant all right," Dreadhorn said, and Isobel looked at him in surprise and confusion.

"Wait, what?" she said. "What does that mean?"

"Merely expressing my belief in your absolute success."

The thick muscled faun looked away from the girl and cast his gaze skyward in hopes of avoiding her eyes, and in doing so, noticed the sun and moon now occupied the same sky. Nether showed any sign of letting the other go past.

"We'd better get started," he said.

He smiled at Isobel in a broad and completely insincere way she had become all too familiar with. She knew him showing her his teeth might just as well have meant he was about to bite her. The blonde-haired girl also knew, in all certainty, he lied through them.

Chapter 17

Redheart and Karl the barman stood in the grand foyer of Winterbourne asylum, completely alone and in total silence but for the loud, incessant hammering of the second hand of a massive, decrepit clock on the far wall.

"Do you think we're early?" the faun asked in striped pyjama bottoms.

"Early for what? It's a nut house, not a bridge club. It's not as though there's a time to go crazy, is there? Oh, nine o'clock everyone, time to start flinging poo and cackling madly."

"Where do you suppose everyone is, then?"

"Well it's quite obvious," Karl said, clucking at his friend's ignorance. "It's only eight forty-five, everyone must still be bathing."

"What, all at once?"

A klaxon sounded and rows and rows of doors along the hallways that exited off of the grand foyer swung open. With little warning than that, it became the gathering place for the seething cauldron of madness that was the two hundred odd inmates of Winterbourne Asylum, with a small horned man in striped pyjama bottoms and a slightly pudgy, greasy-haired barman standing in the eye of the storm.

For the most part, the walking unglued of Winterbourne, all wore white hospital gowns. To call them clean white gowns would have stretched the meaning of the word beyond nearly all reasonable interpretations. Some wore personal touches, grey cardigan sweaters, Blood red beaded crucifixes, and rough woolen hats, no doubt provided by family members in an effort to keep them in touch with a world that was all but invisible to them, and altogether confounding.

"Snootchy!" the tall thin man with long, blonde hair trailing down from beneath his balaclava said. "Me and you mother, huh? Huh? Huh? Bunggggg! Snootchy bootches!" And he disappeared back into the maelstrom of madness that whirled around the two of them.

They were all clean shaven and shorn with a few exceptions, like the man in the ski mask, and they walked in a continual, stagnating spiral to the left. From an unseen speaker, a scratchy recording of the farmer in the dell blared and Karl thought the whole tableau began to look like a ghastly game of musical chairs played by the living dead.

"Where should we look?" Karl asked.

"What?" the faun barked. "This was your idea. You said you knew where she was, remember?"

"I said I knew where she was. I didn't say I knew what bloody room she was in."

"Convenient."

The farmer was near to taking a wife when the crowd sensed something was about to happen and began to move away from the exits of the grand foyer. From out of the centre most hallway emerged a tall, thin nurse in a starched white uniform who walked in short, darting motions like a bird turning over stones on the beach looking for specks of dropped lunches. Behind her walked a tall, salt and pepper haired orderly with pale blue eyes wheeling a cart.

"Okay Ezra," she squawked. "Line them up."

"You heard the lady," Ezra Schneider barked. "Line up for meds."

The inmates dutifully formed into a single line and stepped forward to the nurse with mouths open.

"I'm not taking any of that," Redheart whispered.

"Me either," Karl said. "But if we move out of this line we'll get buckled for sure."

The two slowly started slipping behind inmate after inmate, making their way to the back of the line. Figuring the furthest point from the hawkeyed nurse and her morose looking orderly, offered the greatest chance of avoiding a good pilling up.

"I wouldn't take those pills if I were you," a voice from behind them said. "They make you go all funny for days."

Karl spun around expecting to meet the owner of the voice face to face, only to find the words came from much lower down. Behind him stood a fair complicated woman with shoulder length, silver hair wearing a starched white hospital gown and green striped pyjama bottoms. Two delicate, wheat-coloured horns extended gracefully from her temples.

"Well, you'd be Mavis Draper's boy," she said.

"Yes, but how would…" Karl stammered.

Redheart turned quickly and faced the other faun with a smile.

"A lot of our folk have been looking for you," he said.

"Well, let 'em look," she said.

"The two of you had better come with me," the elder faun said. "Keep your heads down and your mouths shut."

She led the two of them to a small room that was one of three down a hallway at the rear of the grand foyer. The tiny faun pushed on the heavy steel door that revealed a sparsely decorated room with a small single bed and an equally small table and chair, but relative to its occupant's size, it was a king-sized suite.

"How did you find me?"

"Karl figured it out."

"I always told your mother you were much too clever for a human child. A bit of faun in you somewhere, I bet."

"We need your help," Redheart said, coming straight to the point.

"Ah, James. My help is always needed. Trouble is, there's almost never enough needing to do the actual giving of the help."

"Wait, what?" Redheart gasped, feeling as though the scrap of rug he stood on had suddenly just been yanked from under him. "Don't you even want to hear what it is first?"

"I'm sorry, boys." She smiled in a grandmotherly way. "I'm not interested. Whatever it is."

EIGHTEEN

Isobel sat in the shadow of a huge box elder tree and watched Dreadhorn put piles of dried sticks and bits of moss together to make a fire. After several unsuccessful attempts involving bashing two fist sized chunks of stone together and blowing toward the resulting sparks until he nearly collapsed from light headedness, she stood and moved to help him.

"You're doing that wrong."

"I am sergeant at arms and high protector to his majesty Lucerne III king of all fauns. I assure you, I am not doing it wrong," he sneered.

"All right," she said, doing her best to disguise the satisfied grin and leaned back against the big tree.

After a quarter of an hour passed, she began to feel the cold in the air. She walked over and took the flint from the ground beside him.

"Go gather some small sticks," she said to him. "As many as you can carry."

"That sounds suspiciously like an order. Don't, even for a second, pretend to think that–"

"You want to freeze tonight or stay warm by a nice fire?"

The powerful faun stared at her through eyes ringing with contempt and for a moment, considered telling the girl what he thought of her nice bloody fire. But the fact was in the few minutes since he'd stopped banging away at the flint, Dreadhorn became quite aware another cold night was fast descending, and the thought of a warm fire did sound rather nice. He stood to find sticks.

"Have you got a knife?" she asked him as he walked past.

Dreadhorn handed her a small, black handled knife with an ornate silver cap at the end of it and disappeared into the brush. The girl drew the knife from its sheath and scraped the edge downward against the flint, sending a steady stream of bright, fat sparks pouring onto the pile of dried moss. The sparks caught quickly, and soon a thin plume of smoke rose up from the tinder. Isobel directed a few slow and steady breaths at the bottom of the smouldering pile and it burst into flame.

Dreadhorn appeared with an arm full of twigs and slightly larger sticks which Isobel arranged carefully onto the burning moss until she was certain the flame would last. After a time, and with unwavering confidence, the girl ordered the faun off for bigger pieces and a few logs to keep the flame burning through the night.

Isobel took the small parcel out of her pack and unwrapped the chunks of smoked rat meat. She felt the memory of the awful grey lumps effervescing along the back of her tongue and the nausea rose in her throat. However, the gnawing and rumbling in her belly was nearly deafening and reminded her she hadn't eaten a thing since she'd stuffed her gob with the rotten stuff too many hours before.

"Wait!" Dreadhorn said with a measure of excitement in his voice. "Wait."

He got up quickly and tromped off into the woods like a faun with a purpose, and returned shortly with, what Isobel would later swear was, a smile on his face. Along with that, he carried a large handful of greenery and a large soup pot with a thin metal handle.

"Where did that pot come from?" Isobel asked.

"From my pack," Dreadhorn replied. "You have the food, I have the utensils to cook it. Did you think we'd eat that horrid, bloody rat meat as it was?"

Isobel felt, for a moment, as angry as she had ever possibly been, but softened a little when a wry smile appeared on the faun's face.

"Had to see if you'd do it." He grinned. "Bit of a larf for the lads and me. We all did it too, as young ones."

The faun took the packet of meat from the girl and put the lion's share of it in the pot along with some of the small green leaves he collected after another jaunt into the woods. He managed to rig up a tee-pee of three thickish green branches and carefully hung the pot from them over the fire. Dreadhorn reached for his pack and produced two wooden bowls and two primitive looking wooden spoons, and passed Isobel one of each before dipping a spoon into the broth. After bringing it to his lips and a thoughtful look or two, decided it needed more greenery.

"Why are you here, girl?" he asked Isobel after a time.

"The king asked me to do this, to save your village for generations to come."

"Yes, yes." Dreadhorn sighed. "We all know why you're here but why are you here?"

The girl thought silently about what the faun really meant and though she already knew the answer, Isobel wasn't sure telling Dreadhorn was the right way to go. He had little use for the child and showed it with almost nothing but contempt, and the few times he'd been passable, she was certain it was only a set up for the next opportunity to chide her. She heard the voice of her father in her head.

"Any idiot can close their eyes, be afraid and run," Ezra said. "Standing still, even with hot fear running down your leg and puddling up at your feet? Now that says something."

"My life is meaningless."

"What?" Dreadhorn chuckled. "Seems a tad insightful for one so young."

"No. Well maybe. My whole life I have been picked on, poked fun of for being poor, for being different."

"Ah," the faun said in mocking sympathetic tones. "Needed to prove we're the same as everybody else, did we? And that even the smallest of us have value, something like that?"

"No, I – I –"

"I'm going to share something very important with you. It's meaningless, all of it. Respect, power, wealth, all these invisible islands of prestige that we're all trying so desperately to get to mean absolutely bugger all. The only thing that ever truly matters is love. At the end of the day, if you can, well and truly, say that you have loved and that you are lucky enough to be loved, then the world will say that you have everything."

Isobel stared at him, mouth slightly open in shock at this bullish, often snide and overbearing, civil servant sitting across from her, stirring a pot of smoked rat stew, and waxing on about the greatest wealth like a heartsick poet. She tried to respond but could only manage a sort of "pnurf" sound before he took her bowl and filled it with stew.

"What do you love, girl? A fuzzy bear or some other such trinket no doubt."

"I love you," Isobel said matter-of-factly.

"Me?" an instantly embarrassed faun asked.

"Full of ourselves out in the forest, are we?" she asked him. "Not just you, your kind."

"What do you mean?"

"I was trying to say before that I have always been made fun of for being different, but I don't mind. I am different. I'm different today, and I will be different tomorrow, and the day after that until I become a very different old lady who dies and is buried in a very different grave. If I never do another thing from this day to that, nothing will ever change."

"Is there a point to all of this?"

"If I decide not to do this one thing, difficult or easy, all of you will die in a matter of time because I chose not to be different. And then being different really will have earned everyone's ridicule."

It was his turn to stare in stunned silence. He took a handful of dirt from beside him, brought it to his face and breathed deeply.

"We should sleep," he said gruffly, and threw a fat log on the fire. "There's a storm rolling toward us and we should be moving before it hits."

"Good idea."

Isobel made her bed roll as comfortable as possible, and examined her pocket to make sure the three travellers were still all right. After attesting to their safety and stuffing a little rat meat in her pocket for them, she laid down, thinking she was tired enough to sleep on the top of a picket fence if it came right down to it. In minutes, the exhaustion overtook her.

Dreadhorn contemplated the small black knife she'd used to get the fire going – pulled it from its sheath, and stared at the prone figure across from him. It was less than half a day's journey from here and Lucerne was counting on him to get her to the fountain in short order.

"There are already too many of them in that bloody town," he muttered to himself. "One fewer won't matter once it's all finished."

Dreadhorn pulled the fringes of the bedroll up close to stave off the chill of the night air, never once taking his eyes off Isobel, nor his hand off the knife.

NINETEEN

The carved entryway initially appeared as small as the room they left though, now that they had candle light inside of it, they could see it as more of a tunnel than a room.

"No," sneered the priest. "No, this isn't at all creepy."

The hallway began to narrow and lower. Soon they were single file and on hands and knees, edging slowly through it.

"Can you see anything?" Father Brennan asked.

"Dark," Tom said. "And it smells close, musty, like it stops somewhere just ahead."

"Did you just say that you can smell the size of a room?" the priest asked.

They edged a bit farther and, in fact, came to a room that did smell a bit musty. Brennan eyed the gardener suspiciously. The room, by comparison to the spaces they just left, was cyclopean in size. Clearly designed in a manner similar to the small room at the other end of the tunnel, thick, carved stone walls that might have once been painted white to appear more welcoming, but were now yellowed with years of dirt and dust. The similarity ended there, however.

By the dim candlelight, the two could make out a large wooden table along the left wall, above which hung and old kerosene lamp. Tom took a hold of it and shook gently.

"Full!" he said excitedly, and pushed a candle onto its wick.

He held the lamp up and saw several others hanging at various spots around the room. One by one he lit them, and soon the whole room glowed in a slightly spectacular, oil fumed daylight.

With the room lit up like high mass, Tom and Father Brennan could see this was no stone box, this was a room meant to be occupied by the living, and meant to offer as many comforts as one could get in a tomb. The large wooden table along the left wall, on closer examination, revealed itself to be a grandly ornate writing desk with a high-backed leather chair beside it. Along the facing wall, a large, cherry wood chesterfield with thick, red upholstery, and an overstuffed chair and coffee end-table along the other.

Father Brennan stood, basking in the room's glow and whistled.

"Some kinda weird in here," the priest mused.

"Father," Tom gasped. "Look!"

Directly to the right of the priest was a large, deep, pantry with glass doors that, with a bit of wiping, he could clearly see tins of food through.

"Do you suppose it's safe?" he asked.

"I think old man Winterbourne meant to keep folks out of here. I think this place was meant for him and him alone. It's a good bet the food is perfectly edible."

Father Brennan looked carefully at the pantry, his mind flooded by visions of soft hands being pierced by all manner of nasty, poison tipped spikes as he tried to open it.

"I don't suppose I can get you to do this?" he asked the older man.

"Pffft," Tom blew. "Not bloody likely."

"Right," Brennan said. "I'll just say a little prayer of delivery, shall I?"

"If you think it'll help," Tom chuckled.

Father Brennan raised a trembling hand and grabbed the small brass knob. Knob, he thought. What a stupid word knob, knob, blob, bob, glob. He covered all of the rhyming words that immediately came to his mind and was no nearer to actually opening the door. This is the very type of thing meant to test one's faith. But what is tested when you have no faith?

"Right. Here we go."

"So you've said."

Father Brennan closed his eyes and pulled on the doorknob, wincing against the imminent arrival of searing pain before his mind had a chance to mull around the utter meaninglessness of cupboard hardware again.

"It's locked," he exhaled, fairly certain he wouldn't need a change of trousers. "Try to find a key."

Tom shot him a blank look.

"The desk," Brennan said in frustration. "Look in the God damned desk."

Tom slid open the centre drawer of the writing desk and after moving several small stacks of paper, found two small steel keys. He tossed them to the priest who then resumed his introspective vigil in front of the pantry.

"I've never heard of a key setting off a trap," Tom said. "Might be a tad dangerous for the owner of the keys, no?"

"That's stupid," Father Brennan said, almost automatically.

But he had to admit, even if it was only silently to himself, it made perfect sense. The key fit the keyhole and the panty door opened. No venomous daggers sprung forth, nobody even jumped out to call him a nasty name. What he found instead were rows and rows of food, glorious food. Tins of baked beans and potatoes and peas and all the other mundane foods that had ever been canned and wound up in pantries all over the world, but there were also things he had never even heard of, let alone consumed. Escargot with shallots in white wine sauce, smoked Atlantic eels and pate de fois gras. As his gaze moved further down the pantry, it became apparent old man Winterbourne's tastes ranged from the banal to the downright bizarre.

"Ahhh," Brennan said with relish. "How about a drink, Tom?"

The priest turned to the gardener, cradling a fifth of fifteen-year-old malt whisky in each arm.

"Pass me a bottle," Tom said. "And a tin of anything, I'm starving."

A little more rooting around in the desk produced a tin opener, and soon they were well fed and well drunk, lounging on furniture that was nearly as luxurious as the food. Tom held up his bottle, feeling a small twinge of remorse, that in two or three swallows, he would be completely paralytic.

"Why did you become a priest?" he asked the older man.

"Why did you become a gardener?" the priest spat back.

"My father was the head gardener at the Winterbourne estate when I was a boy," Tom said bluntly. "And I would tag along with him. Once in a while, he'd let me help out. He found I had a knack for it, so he started to teach me all he knew."

"Really?" the priest sneered. "You come to this by some kind of birthright?"

"No," Tom said barely concealing his sarcasm. "Do you think that gardening is some kind of family legacy?"

Father Brennan stared at him blankly.

"I worked in the mill after the war. Thirty years I spent inside that place, and after I retired, I couldn't seem to keep still. My missus suggested volunteering down at the church. Good way to cleanse the soul, she called it and my soul was plenty dirty after the war. After she died, the flowers were all I had left."

"And here I was expecting some hard luck story about a promise to a dying mother to keep the begonias alive at the church just the way she used to."

"Nothing so…"

"Or something a tad more salacious," the priest continued. "Like what you and Mrs. Kiel used to get up to behind the holly hock bushes, kind of thing."

Tom emptied his whisky bottle and walked to the pantry with his head bowed. He stood over the priest in silence, and it occurred to him how mind-bendingly simple it would be to kiss the full whisky bottle upside the priest's cranium and make his way back to the church, bolting the door as he went. The older man imagined the arrogant young man waking in the pitch-dark mausoleum, calling out to the empty blackness and slowly losing his mind as he accepted he had nothing left but to wait for death to take him.

"What?" the priest asked.

"What, what?" Tom asked.

"You're smiling, what are you smiling at?"

"Oh, thinking of Mrs. Kiel in the Holly hock bushes."

Father Brennan emptied his own bottle and stood, swaying as he did so, and began to look around the room.

"This can't be it," he said.

"Can't be what?" Tom asked.

"The secret is in the trees, Tom," the good father slurred. "No bloody trees underground, Tom."

He began to wander around the room, moving from place to place searching for any sign of something less disappointing than the truth that A. H. Winterbourne was a complete nutter. He walked back to the doorway they had come in and tried to push the pantry one way and then the other, hoping it would trigger a door of some kind. It was bolted to the floor and wouldn't budge. He to the back wall and began to rap his knuckles on it, hoping for a hollow sound somewhere along it. The priest came away with bloody knuckles and the feeling he'd read far too many mystery stories as a boy.

"Aaaaagh... hey."

He raised his head up to release a scream of anguish and frustration, and noticed a hollow shaft in the ceiling that was currently allowing a thin beam of moonlight to enter the room. Looking around the stone room, he saw three mirrors, each beside one of the kerosene lamps that hung on the walls of the room.

Tom walked over, and stood below the moonlight shaft.

"It's getting brighter," he said. "We need to find something to get the moonlight to these mirrors."

"That's a bit far-fetched," Father Brennan sighed. "This isn't a fairy story."

Tom spied an old swivel mirror sitting on the writing desk and after silently noting the irony of finding exactly what he needed at a time when he needed it most, walked back to the shaft. He could see the moon clearly now, and tilted the mirror until it caught the reflection and sent a beam careening toward the mirrors, bouncing from one to the next until the light finally rested on the far wall, highlighting a small door knob about an inch from where the priest had stopped knocking. He made his way to it and turned back to the priest who stood motionless, mouth agape in complete amazement.

"Son of a…"

"It's unlocked," Tom said, and pulled the heavy stone door open.

The door opened into another hallway, bathed in dazzling, emerald green light.

The hallway looked fairly short, although the priest was in no hurry to get to the end of it, making it seem that much longer. At the end of it he could see the outline of a door that seemed to be the source of the odd green light. To his surprise, it wasn't a door so much as it was a curtain. Sheer like the draperies that hung everywhere in the rectory, though not as flimsy.

Father Brennan stuck out his hand to touch it and instantly felt himself being pulled toward the opaque valance. He recoiled in shock, pulling his arm securely against his chest, but after a second thought, he reached it back out again. His hand began to vanish through the curtain, though he could see it clearly on the other side. The pull became stronger, and soon his elbow moved through, followed by his shoulder. In a blink, he stood on the other side of the curtain surrounded by trees and looking back down at the hallway toward the stone door, and hoping Tom hadn't already packed it in.

"The secret is in the trees," he said.

TWENTY

"How can you do this?' Redheart shouted.

"Lower your voice, or they'll come in here and make you take those pills," the old faun said. She rolled her eyes back and let her tongue loll out of her mouth, feigning madness.

"How can you turn us away like this, so easily, so carelessly?" Redheart contested.

"Try to understand, James. It's not as though I was ever going to help you."

"Wait, what?"

"You're quite a lovely faun, James Redheart, really you are, but I'm not interested in helping you. Honestly couldn't give a turnip's about why you've come."

"But the black sun!" he cried.

"It's always something, dear," she said in a maternal, I love you but keep your feet off of the sofa kind of way. "Black sun rising, blue suede shoes being stepped on, girls not taking a chatting up the way they should. Somebody always wants something, and generally speaking, they want it free of charge."

Redheart groped blindly for the chair and collapsed into it as soon as he found it.

"But I don't…"

"Look, it's all very simple. A very long time ago I turned away from the fauns of Na Doireachan."

"But why?" Redheart asked.

"Because they have lost their way," she spat. "Then as now."

"I don't follow."

"Oh dear, shall I draw you a diagram?"

"Well I..." Redheart trailed off dejectedly.

They sat in silence for a time, the three of them neither wanting to say what they all were feeling. An impasse had been reached and any hope James Redheart and Karl the barman had of averting the impending cataclysm faded like frost on the trees of an early spring morning.

"Lucerne means to make war on the humans," Redheart blurted in desperation.

"And?" the old one asked. "Is that all?"

"Isn't it enough?" the younger faun shouted in desperation. "The black sun is rising in the sky, Lucerne means to live up to the legends and decimate the humans. This is all very, very bad. Isn't that all enough to get you to help?"

"Umm..." She thought for a moment. "Well, no."

"What?"

"Your generation always wants. What's in it for me? Will the girls like it if I do this? Nothing changes and it surely won't stop even if I do help."

Redheart leaned back and covered his face with both hands.

"You're not seeing the—"

"Can I interrupt?" Karl asked, cutting off the faun.

Redheart had all but forgotten the presence of his friend in his single-minded bid to get the old one to help them.

"Maybe we're thinking about this the wrong way."

"What do you mean?" the elder faun asked.

"Well, it seems to me that we don't actually need you to help, per se."

"Wait," Redheart said.

"What?" said the old one.

"No really," Karl said. "Beyond opening a door, what do we really need her for? No offence, ma'am."

"None taken."

"Once the door is open, James and I can find this girl, and then the Lucerne problem should, more or less, sort itself out, no?"

"What girl?" the old one asked, the tone of her voice sounding suddenly grave.

Redheart sighed and lowered his head.

"I had hoped to keep that one a little closer to the vest until the time was right."

"Who is the girl?" the old one asked again.

"Sorry," Karl said sincerely. "I didn't know it was a secret."

"Who is the girl?" the old one asked through ever growing impatience.

"No matter," Redheart said hopefully. "She was bound to find out soon enough."

The room began to shake and the walls looked as though they were moving in on them, like some large and choleric hand squeezed the room like an empty box of scotch mints, hoping that enough shaking might produce just one more. The lights in the room began to flicker and what little brightness had filtered in through the dirty white linens that covered the 'small window, suddenly grew dim.

"James Cagney Redheart!" the tiny old faun bellowed in a voice that sounded twelve feet high. "I am a child of the first and I am no fool to be bandied about with."

The young faun felt a constriction around his chest and saw thick, green tendrils reaching from a potted plant stretching out at him and wrapping around his wrist and forearm with an unbelievable ferocity, squeezing him for all it was worth.

"Who is the girl?" the old one demanded.

"I believe that she is," Redheart said as the plant wrapped around his chest and tightened its earthy grip. "Ungh… that she is…"

The elder faun took on a glow that made her look much larger than she was, as though she had stretched and expanded, and now filled the whole of the room. Redheart resisted telling her anything else as long as he was able, but as the vines began to constrict around him, tighter and tighter, he felt he'd better give the old faun something or she'd pop him out of his skin like a grape.

"She is the child of nature!" he gasped.

"You what?" the old one asked, shaking her head in disbelief.

The elderly faun returned to her former sway-backed, stooping self and rolled her arms and shoulders as if shaking herself loose from the last traces of monstrous, glowing presence she had been.

"You know, I must be much more of an old goat than I thought. I could've sworn you just said she was the child of nature."

Redheart found himself more than a little intimidated by the old faun and afraid to speak now. He nodded his head slowly then lowered it, keeping his eyes firmly fixed on the ground below his hoofs. Feeling as though he'd just been scolded.

"How do you know it's her, what makes you so certain?"

"I've been following her for a very long time, years in fact. There's no doubt in my mind that it's her."

"And she had no idea you were following her?" the old faun asked.

"Not so far as I know."

"Impressive," she said.

"Creepy," Karl added.

The two fauns shot a look of confusion at their human counterpart.

"What?" Karl asked. "I'm sure this is okay for you lot, but on the other side of the trees, following a person for a year makes you a fuzzy legged stalker. People get locked away for that kind of thing."

The old one paid no heed to the barman's words. "Still, following around a human doesn't prove anything."

"The three are with her," Redheart said without hesitation.

"For how long?"

"Almost from the beginning."

"The three what?" Karl asked.

"Does it matter?" the old faun asked.

"Not particularly," Karl answered. "Just feeling a bit left out."

"Where is the girl now?"

"Headed for the fountain," Redheart said. "Likely with Dreadhorn."

The wizened old faun sat at the table and looked back and forth between Karl and Redheart.

"I will open the door for you," she sighed. "But I will go no farther than that."

"Agreed," Redheart said. "We can handle it from there."

"No, James," the old one said earnestly. "Once the door is open, you will be on your own. Karl cannot go with you."

"What?" screeched a shocked barman. "What do you mean Karl cannot go with him?"

"It was a faun who created the rift between our kind and yours and it must be a faun to heal it."

"Everybody can use a hand from time to time," Karl suggested hopefully.

"Yes," the elder faun agreed. "But not this time Karl. I will give Redheart all that he needs. I will pour all of my knowledge into him before I let him pass through the door."

"Well yes," Karl stuttered. "Yes, good. Yes, I'm sure that will be good too."

Karl looked awkwardly at his friend, unsure what to say to him now that his part in this adventure had come to an abrupt and wholly inglorious end.

"You're going to see me off, aren't you?" Redheart asked.

"Yeah," Karl said, nearly inaudibly.

"What?" Redheart said.

"Yes," Karl said quite loudly now. "I'll bloody see you off. All right?"

"Wonderful," the old one said. "Would you two like a moment alone or can we go to the door now?"

TWENTY-ONE

"We need to do this quickly and quietly," the elderly faun said. "If Ezra catches us, it's going to put him in an awkward position to say the least."

"Ezra?" Redheart asked. "Ezra Schneider?"

"That's the fellow," the old one answered. "Why?"

"It's not important."

"Suit yourself." She shrugged and stuck her head carefully out the doorway of her cell.

"All right, we need to make it to the basement stairs on the other side of the building. I'll open the door down there. We should be all right until we go through the main foyer."

"Through the what?" Redheart asked.

"Through the main foyer."

The old one had made it a point to overemphasize her pronunciation of the word.

"The main foy-err," the elder faun repeated.

Redheart supposed it was an older generational thing or maybe the old girl had been with the humans too long or maybe just didn't care that she was pronouncing the word incorrectly. It was such a small thing, after all, but it grated on his nerves like nothing he'd ever known before.

"Let's just call it the hallway," Redheart suggested.

"What?" she asked. "Call what the hallway?"

"The foy-yay," he said.

"What happens in there?" Karl asked.

"Where?" the old one asked.

"The big room," Karl said.

"This time of day, the foy-err will be full of inmates. So long as we don't draw any attention to ourselves, we should make it through unnoticed."

"How do we go about not drawing attention to ourselves?" Redheart asked.

"By not acting like a lunatic!" the old one answered. "Everybody in this place is well-known to the people that guard it, including their behaviour. Anything out of the ordinary, like two fauns and a grubby barman acting crazy will put eyes on us like stink on a badger."

"Oh, right," Karl said. "Of course."

He threw a look at Redheart that said he wondered what had ever given him the idea that this wizened old faun was ever anything but a complete nut job.

They slipped out of her room and down the hallway into the grand foyer without incident. As they entered the vast room they were, at once, overwhelmed by the dreadful volume of the inmates milling aimlessly around in it. Redheart wondered how anybody, guard or inmate, could possibly spot anything out of the ordinary.

"This should be easy," Redheart said, and he started walking toward the raucous carousel.

"Stop!" she hissed and grabbed hold of his arm. "Ezra has eyes like a hawk and he could hear a cockroach pissing in a rainstorm."

"Colourful," Karl said.

"And dangerous. If anything is going to get us caught, it'll be you acting the goat James Redheart."

Redheart stopped and raised a finger for emphasis, about to make his point crystal clear to her and opened his mouth to speak.

"This isn't like yammering away in Italian for a half-wit of a gate keeper," the old one barked. "Ezra and the nurse and one or two others are the real guards of this place. On a whim, they could have you drugged up and zapped up until you thought you were the daughter of a Belgian chocolatier."

They both turned to her and smiled as any notions they had of her being helpless and feeble vanished before their eyes.

"What is it with you all and foreign cultures?" Karl asked Redheart.

"We have an extensive library of travel brochures," Redheart said.

The three of them walked in silence the rest of the way into a room where silence no longer existed. Every inmate housed in Winterbourne asylum made every noise they were able to make, and all simultaneously.

"It's so loud in here I can't breathe," Karl said. "How do you live with all of this noise all of the time?"

"Shhh, idiot!" She waggled a bony finger at him.

"You get used to it a lot quicker than you'd think. It's that door we need." She pointed to a door all the way on the other side of the room, about two hundred odd feet from where they stood. Between them nine hundred people milled about, each one of them mad as a March hare.

"Keep your heads down," the old faun whispered. "And your mouths shut.

They stepped into the fray and followed along in the endless circle the inmates all walked, constantly looking for a chance to make a break and move toward the cellar door. The tall thin man Redheart encountered on their way in, came up to them and spoke to the elder faun in calm and familiar tones.

"Noich!" he hollered at her.

"Not now," she said. "We've got to see the director."

"Oh," he said. "The director, eh? Tell him I'm ready for my close up."

He produced a small silver tube from the pocket of his bath robe and began applying lipstick as though he were a child scribbling spirals on a piece of paper.

"My close up!" he screamed. "Michael, I'll be in my trailer."

"Come on you two," she said.

They'd managed to make it halfway across the room when several of the inmates began to crowd around them, chanting and pointing at Redheart.

"What's going on?" Karl asked.

"Damn," she said. "I should have told him."

"Told him what?" Redheart asked with panic rising in his voice.

"It's your hat dear," she said. "They want your hat."

"You're kidding," Karl said. "They're getting this worked up over a floppy gardening hat?"

"Lunatics, they don't really know what they want. James darling, just take it off and toss it away. It'll be fine, there's a good lad."

"What's with you?" Karl asked. "Darling, good lad?"

"Calming tones, impudent dolt, calming tones. If we speak calmly, they stay calm and we get through is in one piece."

Redheart pulled off his hat and reached his arm back to toss it far off to his right. When he finally pitched the hat, a group of the disturbed rushed forward and began grabbing for it, pushing the faun back as they moved and he vanished beneath a frothing mass of eager arms and gnashing teeth.

Karl lost sight of his friend and attempted to join the ruckus and locate the faun until he too was pulled down in the tide of fixated madmen. There was a strange smell of the new and unfamiliar about the three of them and it whipped the inmates into a frenzy like sharks ravening around fresh blood in the water.

"Stop this at once!" the old one yelled, but they were all far too gone to be satisfied by anything now but bloodshed.

"Come here, rabbit," a gangly creature of a man with goggle eyes and grey, rotting teeth hissed at Redheart.

The small faun tried to push his way clear but there were just too many pairs of hands clawing at him, trying to rip him to bits. The grey toothed man-thing weaseled and snaked his way through the cat's cradle of arms holding the faun down and put his own arms securely around James Redheart's throat. Karl the barman reached out to help his friend, only to feel dozens of hands on his own arms, wringing and twisting near to their breaking point. He dropped to his knees and closed his eyes.

The elder faun walked to the middle of the crowd of wilding lunatics, in an effort to calm them and persuade them back to a place that resembled some sense of humanity.

"Come children," she soothed. "Come now, let's not–" and was suddenly interrupted by mad flailing of arms that now had a hold of her too.

Karl the barman pushed his way forward, toward the elderly faun and punched and kicked as many as he could, trying to staunch the flow of hundreds of maniacs, but in an instant he was down again. Redheart's hands shot upward to protect his neck but not quickly enough as he felt the warm, sweaty fingers of the goggle-eyed man seeking a path around the back of his neck and beginning to squeeze when they had found their way there.

Heat rose in his body and gravity left his head. He attempted to find his travelling companions, but good sense told him moving around would give the hands around his neck the opportunity to tighten their feverish grip. The encroaching light-headedness told him travelling companions were highly overrated anyway and the best thing to do now was just lie back and let the syrupy waves of blackness splash over him. Redheart saw the lights dim and heard the long, whistling screech of a grackle. He closed his eyes and let the blackness take him.

The faun had the sensation of falling at an incredible speed but it also seemed that time crawled by as he fell. Redheart closed his eyes and felt nearer somehow to the end of his plummet and prepared for the sickening crunch of his own body as it impacted with the solid ground.

The crunch didn't arrive. Instead, the small body slowed, nearly to a stop and landed upright, virtually where it had first fallen under the hands of the gangly thing with the dingy teeth. He gently removed the hands of the lunatic and placed them slightly to the right of where they had been around his throat and stood.

They were frozen-all of them. Karl and the old one, every lunatic and every guard and nurse, hard as a carp, as though they were all wind-up toys that had just suddenly run down. Time, it seemed, had stopped or so he thought, until he heard the thunderous clack of the big clock's second hand.

"Just moving very slowly," the voice said.

"What?" Redheart asked.

From a dimly lit hallway to the little faun's left, emerged a small faun, who bore an incredible resemblance to his father. The new faun wore a black velvet waistcoat with a delicate, silver watch chain stretched across its front and bore a kindly expression that instantly put Redheart at ease.

"You're not?"

"No," the faun said. "It's often easier this way, seeing someone familiar."

His face began to fade and shimmer until it looked like a shapeless, reflective pool of liquid silver.

"Um," Redheart said.

"Oh," the faceless faun said. "It doesn't always stay in the beginning, just a moment.

He stuck his thumb between his lips and began to blow, and like a balloon slowly inflating, the face of Redheart's father appeared again.

"Am I dead? Is that why you're here?"

"No, not dead," the faun said. "But that is why I'm here. If you were dead, some rather nasty, lizardy looking characters would have come for you."

The clock let go another bone-rattling clack.

"Come, take a walk outside with me," the small faun said.

They walked past the torpid occupants of the grand foyer, out the front doors, and onto the steps that led down to the street. Halfway down the big stairs lay a generous granite landing with a cobblestone path leading away from it and around to the back of the building, ending at a small flower garden with a stone bench in the centre of it.

"Nice here, huh?"

"Yes," Redheart agreed. "Lovely."

"Very few know about this place, fewer still visit it."

"It's really very nice. I would love to spend my days here pruning and preening and taking care of all the things that grow and stretch and creep and crawl. Look, what is this all about?"

"You could have this," he said. "All the time. You could come and sit here in the peace and quiet, maybe water the flowers from time to time, though they don't need it, strictly speaking. And no one would ever come here except the ones who are waiting."

"Waiting for what?"

"For someone to show them where they are to go from here."

"And that would be me?" Redheart asked.

"You always were quick, James."

The little faun in the black waistcoat clapped his hand on Redheart's shoulder and a wave of warmth and ardour radiated over him like a kiss on the forehead from his mother on a rain drenched Sunday afternoon.

"But I…"

"I'm offering you a choice," the other faun said. "One that most don't get. "You're here already, the hard part is done. Take my hand and you can stay here and help those who will need it."

Redheart looked at his hand, turning it over and back again, admiring it for all the strength that lay within it. He began to reach out to the faun.

"Wait," he said, pausing mid reach. "What about the girl, what will happen to her if I stay here?"

"I wish I could say that you staying here will buy her some kind of mercy on the other side, but that kind of thing only happens in stories. If you stay here, Isobel will come to this garden, it is only a question of when and how."

"And if I go back?" Redheart asked.

"That one is out of my hands. You going back could save her and help her succeed or you could fail miserably and you'd both wind up here anyway."

"Not much of a choice, is it?"

"All choices carry the weight of the world. Good, bad, it all comes down to how far you're willing to go to carry out the choices you make."

"I won't get this chance again, will I?"

"Once in a lifetime sort of thing."

"It is a lovely garden." Redheart stood to leave. "Any tips at all?"

"Help will come to you behind blue eyes. Look to them and ask for it."

The faun in black began to flicker again and soon his whole body shimmered like molten silver.

"Oh," he added. "And wait at least an hour after you eat before you go swimming," he said.

"But I can't swim."

"All the more reason." He disappeared.

Redheart didn't feel like he was falling now so much as he felt like he'd been fired from a cannon. He felt a bulging in his eyes, no doubt from his consciousness bouncing off the inside of his skull at terminal velocity, and he heard the same shrill scream from the same damnable grackle as he became aware of an unfamiliar voice calling out."

"All right you God-damned crazies, let him up and give him some bastarding air," Ezra barked.

A face came into Redheart's view, gaunt and tired and topped with hair more salt than pepper and possessed of the bluest eyes he believed he'd ever seen.

"I need to get to the basement," Redheart said.

"And I need to run for president," Ezra said.

"Please, Ezra, I'm trying to help your daughter."

Ezra stopped cold. The mere mention of his missing daughter would earn you a heavy hand across the jaw in the normal run of things. But there was something about this weird little thing that told him thins was about as far from the normal run of thing as you could get without being fitted for a jacket that does up in the back.

The intercom crackled to life and crashed through the tense quiet like thunder rattling an old window.

Ezra Schneider, please come to the director's office. Ezra Schneider, please come to the director's office.

The older man released his grip on the little thing and stood.

"I don't know you and I didn't see you. Any of you," he said looking at the three of them.

The caretaker reached up on one of the stone walls and pulled the thin cotton rope that dangled below the dull and worn, red bell. A klaxon rang out, bringing a handful of men in white uniforms into the big room to wrangle the inmates, that outnumbered them nearly ten to one, back to their cells. The ensuing pandemonium of guards attempting to herd the insane became a dismal rodeo of embarrassment and failure and it was just the distraction Ezra hoped it would be.

Ezra Schneider to the director's office please, Ezra Schneider to the director's office please. The intercom blared again.

"Get where you need to go. Quickly," he said and started up the stairs toward the director's office.

He stopped midway and turned back, just in time to see Redheart, the Old One and Karl the barman, disappear down the steps into the basement of Winterbourne.

TWENTY-TWO

Isobel walked until she was far enough away from any danger, real or imagined, posed by Dreadhorn. She spied a berm a short distance away with a thick oak log stretched across it. Sitting down on the log and, for the first time since she'd followed the voice from the storm cellar, Isobel began to consider that somewhere along the way, somebody had made a colossal error in choosing her for all of this.

What was once a raging inferno of confidence, thinking she would simply walk into the water below the fountain, snatch up the red plant, and save the three young fauns playing on the grass, now was reduced to a smoking ruin. And what remained was a frightened little girl who really hadn't a clue how to save herself, let alone all of the fauns in this forest. And when it came right down to it, she just missed her father.

"I don't know what to do," she said and could feel the sting of the gathering tears. "I don't know what to do and they're all going to disappear."

Isobel thought, if only for a moment, she might be all right with letting them disappear from the forest, and perhaps the world, but for the laughter in the eyes of the faun children looking up at her from their playground on the lush carpet of grass in the village. She knew then that there really was no choice at all.

The girl looked skyward to the high branches of the tallest trees and hoped that another voice, another creature, might come to her and offer some kind of counsel. When, after five full minutes of scanning the tree line, nothing arrived and no solution of her own presented itself, she stood and began to walk toward the fountain again.

"Oh bugger," she said.

The interior of Seonagh's woods unfolded before her, lush and green, and the thick beams of sunlight streaking in between the leaves and branches kept it warm. But from the pale, washed-out blueness of the sky, she knew it should be snow covered by now.

"All right, living goat-people and all, it stands to reason that the rules don't apply in here," Isobel said.

She'd been following a path of sorts that abruptly split off in three directions ahead of her.

"Ummm, now what?" she wondered.

She felt the wriggling in her pocket and saw three whiskered noses followed by three furry brown heads poke out one by one.

"Well?"

"Squeak," the largest of the three said.

"There are three of you after all, why don't you each go look at one and come back and tell me?"

The three scurried down her arm and looked up from between her feet when she a voice come from deep inside her head, and even deeper within the forest, all at once. It encompassed her in a way that overwhelmed but didn't frighten, as though there were a gigantic amount of power behind the voice and equal measures of warmth and compassion that came along for the ride. It wasn't the voice from the basement, full of sickly sweet words to entice and hypnotic compliments; this was the voice of calm that heralds a storm. Like an earthquake wrapped in a flannel sheet, its power terrified and soothed as it danced through the girl's mind.

"You're a clever girl," the voice said.

"Oh, if I'm so clever, why am I standing here completely lost?" Isobel asked.

"You're not lost," the voice said. "Your head disagrees with what your heart knows to be true."

"How's that?"

"If you had to pick one path right now, which would you choose?" The question echoed around her head.

"I'd go down the left path," Isobel said without hesitation.

"Off you go then."

"What's down there?"

"Only what you take with you," the voice said.

"Wait, what! Am I supposed to bring something with me? Because I haven't."

"No... I mean..." the voice said with confidence that faded quickly. "Wait, what?"

"You said the only thing down the path is what I take with me, does that mean I'm supposed to take something down there with me?"

"Well no. I was implying that this was a journey of discovery, and the only things you would need are you and your cleverness."

"Does nobody say what they mean around here? You all talk in riddles, as though there were some huge secret to hide, but there isn't. These are all very plain, ordinary things to do. Being vague about things doesn't make them any more mysterious, it just makes the let-down that much bigger when they turn out to be ordinary."

"Ah, yes well," the voice pushed on. "I will be with you the whole way, of course, and you needn't be worried.

"Naturally. I haven't had a lot of luck with voices in my head lately, so you'll forgive me if I'm not thrilled about going down that path, whether you're with me or not. I don't even know who you are."

"What if I told you I was your inner voice?"

"I would wonder why my inner voice sounded like a much older, complete stranger."

"Oh, very well. I am the first, mother of all fauns of Na Doireachan, and I have come to warn you."

Trepidation crept through Isobel's voice. "Warn me that if I fail the whole village will die? I know this already, it's all I've been thinking about since I agreed to go and get this bloody plant."

"Plant?" the voice asked. "What plant?"

"The plant I'm meant to get at the bottom of the fountain," she answered. "The plant that is going to restore the water supply and save all fauns for future generations."

"Who filled your head with this nonsense?"

"Lucerne," Isobel said. "King of all fauns."

"Rubbish!" the voice said. "There is no plant at the bottom of that pond."

"Lucerne said that the water supply was poisoned. That there was a plant underneath the fountain at the bottom of the pond. A red plant that would save the water supply and countless generations of fauns."

"The fauns of Na Doireachan get their water from the Nyegard. You can't poison a river. The only thing underneath that fountain is the father of all fauns. I know, because I put him there."

"You killed your husband?" a stunned Isobel asked.

"More of a partner than a husband really," the voice muttered. "And he isn't dead, just sort of… dormant."

"Look what's going on here? Who and what are you?"

"Down here," the voice said, and the three mice looked up at Isobel from between her feet.

"You are three small brown mice, are you?"

"No, and yes," the voice said as though Isobel had asked her if she were a small bit of hard, yellow cheese.

"Huh?"

"When my body passed on, my spirit moved on to a temporary home until a suitable vessel was available for permanent residence. These three happened along as the light left my eyes."

"Wait, what? How can three mice equal one spirit?"

"Quite easy really," the voice said.

"It's not a question of difficulty," Isobel argued. "Three is three and one is one and they aren't ever equal. Not ever at all. One gigantic, all-consuming force into three tiny brown field mice, it just doesn't work out."

"Well sometimes you just have to believe the things you are told and go with them," the voice explained. "It keeps things moving along."

Isobel stood in confused silence for a while and got the distinct impression the owner of the voice, three mice or not, was becoming more than a little annoyed at the stubbornness and impudence of teenaged girls.

"Well?" the voice snipped.

"Yes?" Isobel asked.

"Are you taking the left path or aren't you?"

"Oh, right," Isobel said and she began to walk toward the path through the trees.

"Have you ever thought of something larger, like a badger?"

"Just give it a rest, will you," the voice answered. "Have you ever smelled the inside of a badger?"

Isobel walked a short distance and came to a clearing with a small, jerry-built cabin in the middle of it.

"Go in, child," the voice said.

Isobel hesitated.

"Believe that I would not send you into harm's way without making sure you had the tools to keep you safe."

"What is this place?" Isobel asked.

"A tool shed… of sorts," the voice said.

The building seemed awfully small, only slightly taller than she was, and it had the look of a tree fort built by neighbourhood kids out of lumberyard scraps and bits and pieces stolen from construction sites. She pushed forcefully on one of the walls, hoping it might fall over and save her from having to enter the awful place, but it remained firmly defiant and upright. The door, little more than an old, grey woollen army blanket, hung from the frame. She reached out a hand to pull it back but stopped midway and withdrew in hesitation.

"Shall I go in first?" the voice asked sarcastically.

"All right then," Isobel answered with a note of elation in her voice.

The voice grumbled and three small mice trundled past Isobel's feet to disappear under the blanket, and into the blackness of the playhouse. A horrific screech followed by a deafening silence escaped from behind the grey wool barrier and Isobel's arm shot out to throw back the blanket, revealing three, very cute, much unharmed, mice sitting in a beam of sunlight cascading over her shoulder.

"You see," the voice said. "Perfectly safe."

"Not even a little funny."

"Now tell me what you see," the voice said.

"Can't you see it for yourself?"

"Not exactly," the voice said. "I see through the three of them, but they have managed to retain most of who and what they are. I spend my days determining if things are edible, tough enough to gnaw on, or secluded enough to pee on."

"Oh," Isobel said. "I don't know what…"

"You can see why I am looking for more suitable accommodations."

It was cramped inside, and the only light available pushed its way past the pulled-back blanket. Isobel managed to secure it on a bent nail over her head as she ducked and stepped into the room.

The warmth of the shed made Isobel a little nauseated, and the air felt stale and smelled of a fire that had burnt out long ago. Tucked in the far corner of the shed lay a makeshift bed, which was little more than a pile of straw on top of a rickety looking scrap wood frame covered over by another grey, wool blanket and a bundle of rags for a pillow. Along the facing wall and to the right of the bed, a small table and chair stood cobbled together from more scraps. Isobel walked over to the table and found a decent sized stub of a candle and a box of wooden matches. After a few flicks along the edge of the box, the room was drenched in a dull, yellow light.

Posters and placards, emblazoned with the names of giants of the silver screen, covered the walls of the place almost in entirety. Men and women she'd seen on faded movie stills on the walls of the Parker Street Bijou and heard her father casually mention from time to time at the supper table. On the wall directly above the table hung a different sort of poster. Isobel leaned in closer and raised the candle to get a better look. It read:

Messrs. Gimlet and Hogswallow
Present for the enjoyment of all:
The Phantasmagorical G & H Carnival of Wonders
Featuring, From the Wilds of the Subcontinent,
Urisk! The Wild Goat-Man of the Mountains.
You will be Amazed at his feats of Strength.
You will fill with Wonder at his acts of Daring
Your Heart will fill with Joy as he quotes Verse from the
Bard and Writers of great renown without Prompt!

There were three small, circled drawings at the bottom of the poster, each displaying what was obviously a faun, in all of his glory. First hands raised in a dramatic pose fit for reciting balladry with the bearing of a master orator, next, juggling flaming clubs, and the last circle showed him as the elegant gentleman, immaculately dressed, and looking stoic and serious. On the table below the poster sat a photograph in an antiquated cardboard frame nearly identical to the poster's final circled drawing, showing a faun dressed from the waist up in an opulent jacket and waistcoat with a crisp white shirt and silk tie. The eyes of the faun were pale and nearly amber in the photograph's sepia hues.

"What is this place?" Redheart said.

TWENTY-THREE

Father Brennan walked quietly through the underbrush, treading cautiously for fear someone might hear and wonder what he was up to. He made it a good distance, undiscovered and virtually silent, until he tripped over an unseen branch and fell flat on his face, bashing a knee, tearing a shirt sleeve and scraping up his hands for good measure. From that point he didn't walk nearly as quietly and didn't give a rat's ass who knew he was there as he carried on, grumbling loudly with each pained step.

After several more ignominious trips to the forest floor, he decided he just about had enough and nearly turned around to head back to the mausoleum when he heard raised voices coming through the trees just ahead of him. He moved a little further along, remaining hidden in the underbrush and saw to figures standing in a clearing near a small pond with a decorative, white stone fountain in the centre of it.

"Tell me again, Maurice," the first voice said. "How you allowed the human female to escape you?"

Human? What an odd thing to say.

He inched closer to the treeline and crouched low behind a thicket, listening intently as one voice, clearly having some measure of authority, and continued to chide and intimidate the other.

"Ah, yes, well," the second voice said.

"Go on?"

The priest carefully parted the branches of the shrubbery in front of him and let them close back just as carefully, obscuring his vision once more. He rubbed his eyes and wondered for a moment if he might not be sleeping it off somewhere behind Butler's. It certainly wouldn't be the first time; and it certainly wouldn't be the first time he'd been confronted with images this bizarre after a night at the bottom of a bottle.

Father Brennan put his hand in his pocket, dug around for the small box of wooden matches and struck one against the bark of a tree beside him. The match flared to life and he stared into the orange flame and wondered if this might not be a bit excessive.

The priest stubbed the match out against the bare skin of his forearm and bit his bottom lip to stifle the four-letter word that leaped from forearm to brain. The brain decided instantly that, since this clearly was not the result of dreaming, those things through the verge were very likely the secret in the trees that one Mr. A. H. Winterbourne was getting at. If half the wealth he suspected lay in this place, and if he had any hope of getting it, Father Brennan thought he better be getting along and introducing himself to the two goat-looking things on the other side of the bushes.

"Afternoon fellas," he said while stepping through the trees.

The two fauns stood firm, glaring at the figure emerging from the trees while their fingers wrapped tightly around the handles of the blades hanging from their waists.

"Do you know the penalty for defiling this holy place?" Dreadhorn asked.

"Not really," the priest said. "Something nasty one would assume?"

"Yes," Dreadhorn replied. "Instant and immediate death."

"That's not nasty."

"What?" Dreadhorn said.

"That's not nasty at all," the priest answered.

"Stabbing," the puzzled faun bellowed. "Stabbing not nasty?"

"No," the priest said. "It would be over fairly quickly, very little suffering.

"But the blood," Dreadhorn pleaded. "The pain."

"Naw," the priest said. "If you did it the right way, the blood loss would make you feel relaxed and sleepy long before any of the real pain kicked in. It would be like slipping into a nice warm bath after a glass or two of brandy."

Dreadhorn stepped back toward the other faun and the two began a heated discussion involving many words that were exceedingly loud and foreign to Father Brennan, and they did a great deal of gesturing his way.

Father Brennan walked to the two fauns, extending his hand as he moved.

"Winslow Brennan," he said. "I am the priest over at St. Gertrude's."

"Ah yes," Dreadhorn groaned. "The quaint human custom of fondling each other's hands."

He pushed out a limp wristed attempt at a handshake and allowed the priest to squeeze it for a moment in, what could widely be considered, as one of the worst in the history of handshakes. Somewhere between the revulsion of holding hands to cross the street with an uncle who' just sneezed into his palm, and flaccid broccoli. Father Brennan smiled politely and withdrew his hand, turning toward the other faun and extending it out again.

Dreadhorn roared. "How dare you. Have you no idea who you are pushing your grubby purulent flesh toward?"

"Well no. No, not really."

"This is Lucerne the III, king of all fauns and laird of Na Doireachan."

"Is that a fact," the Father smirked. "And you'd be his lackey, would you?"

"Lackey?" the thick-muscled faun screeched. "I am no lackey. I am high protector and sergeant at arms to his majesty!"

"Well, of course you are," Brennan sneered. "Now, getting back to it, you were saying something about a girl?"

"That's none of your concern," Dreadhorn spat. "You're meddling in things you couldn't possibly fathom in that spiralling lump of cheese you lot call a brain."

"Dreadhorn," the taller faun said. "The man is a guest in our lands and we must treat him with the respect befitting such a holy man."

"But your majesty," Dreadhorn whined.

"Maurice, please."

A look flashed across the eyes of the taller faun that made father Brennan think the Devil really did walk along Grey Hollow road, and he was about to speak with him, face to face.

"Now go and fetch the large, leather bound codex from my things. There's a good kid."

As the muscular faun loped off, the king turned toward the priest and gave him a withering look that started at his feet and ended a foot above his head. If Father Brennan had any doubts how the king felt about him while speaking to Dreadhorn, they were swiftly removed by the time he'd looked him over. He knew he was just this side of skinny, gangly some might say, and his complexion would need a fine grit sandpaper to be considered just okay. His eyes were a little dull and usually puffy and reddened from too many nights on the bar stool, but he didn't think he was so off-putting that he deserved to be ogled by one of the billy goats gruff.

I ought to give him a tin can, smack his ass to get him out of my way and be done with it, he thought.

"My dear Father Brennan," Lucerne said.

Winslow Brennan was a little shocked the faun he assumed hadn't been listening to anything he previously said knew his name. And, despite this staggering realization, he still imagined him chewing on a rusty tin can while speaking.

"What brings you to our beloved Na Doireachan?"

"I am…"

"St. Gertrude's as I recall, is on the other end of Winterbourne. What are you doing so far from home?" the king of all fauns said.

The tone of the king's voice dripped with contempt and suspicion of the priest's motives.

"I am following a trail of breadcrumbs," Father Brennan said. "In a manner of speaking."

"Yes?"

"I have recently come across some artefacts belonging to the late founder of our little town," he said, lying through his teeth. "And became fascinated by the lore and legends he laid down in those dusty texts. From there it was a matter of following the trail here."

If fauns were exceptionally dull creatures, it might have ended there; it might have been story enough to grant the priest a pass from further enquiries. As it turns out, fauns are exceptionally bright beings, far more intelligent and advanced than people in a multitude of ways. For instance, a small group of fauns discovered if you use the Nyegard River to turn a large wooden wheel and string bits of stolen copper to it in a line, you could get the lights to stay on all the time. Trouble was, nobody got any sleep after they did it so they took it apart after a week.

"Father Brennan," Lucerne said with a sudden gravity in his voice that frightened the priest a little. "I recall A. H. Winterbourne as a loathsome, avaricious, bag of flesh who wanted nothing more than to line his own pockets. I can't imagine your purposes being any better if it was his trail you followed here."

Father Brennan lowered his head in shame, shame he had been found out, and shame he would likely not walk out of this place with even as much as he had come in with.

"I'm not sure what to say."

"There is nothing to say. Don't offer me reasons wrapped in insincerity, it insults us both."

The priest remained silent as his eyes scanned the treeline, hoping above hope for some break in the conversation that would afford him a chance to escape. And suddenly it presented itself.

"Perhaps we could help out one another," the king of all fauns said.

"Yes," the priest excitedly blurted. "Absolutely, but how?"

"There is a ritual, of course," Lucerne began. "You are familiar with the importance of rituals, I know. This ritual will secure the future of my kind and yours for all of eternity, and it requires a guest participant if you will."

"And that's where the girl comes in?"

"Very good, very perceptive. I can see why they gave you the charge of something as important as St. Gertrude's."

"What do you need me to do?"

"Do you know why A. H. Winterbourne tried to burn down our sacred glade and all of us with it?"

"No," the priest answered. "Nothing I came across ever explained his mania about this place."

The king of all fauns looked skyward and let out a long, slow breath.

"I thought not, he was very good at keeping up appearances. The founder of your beloved town knew that Na Doireachan sits on top of one of the largest silver deposits in the country, and he wanted it all to himself. You find the girl for me and I will reward you beyond your wildest dreams."

Father Brennan gazed at Lucerne and a profane smile spread across his face. He still imagined the king of all fauns chewing on a rusty tin can, but now every bit of him was adorned in silver finery. Thick silver hoops hung from his earlobes, rings on every finger glinted in the sunlight filtering through the canopy of trees, and a wide, opulent belt hung around his waist, just above his fur covered legs.

"Does she need to die?"

"What?" the faun asked.

"The girl," the priest said in dreamy tones. "Does she need to die?"

"Oh look, here comes Dreadhorn." Lucerne remarked. "Let's see if he knows what the big book has to say about that, shall we?"

The shorter of the two fauns walked up and handed a large, dark, lavishly bound book to the king who proceeded to thumb quickly through it until he arrived at the page he sought. He skimmed over the bold handwritten words on the page and smiled to himself.

"Well"–he closed the book with a great thud–"it would seem it doesn't matter one way or the other."

"What doesn't matter?" Father Brennan asked.

Lucerne III, king of all fauns gestured to his sergeant at arms who bowed and passed him the black handled knife that hung from his belt before stepping back and lowering his head.

"What would you say you are, Father," the faun asked. "About one hundred and forty pounds or so?"

"One forty-three."

"Step a little this way, if you wouldn't mind," the king said, moving the priest into a position directly in front of the pond beneath the white fountain.

"The book says it doesn't matter if it is a male or a female."

"Oh?" the priest asked, not certain where the faun was going.

"No, Father," Lucerne said. "I don't need the girl. You'll do nicely."

The king of all fauns drew the blade swiftly and deliberately across the priest's throat and Brennan dropped to his knees in shock.

"But... but... my... reward," he gurgled.

"Rejoice," the faun cried. "And be glad, for your reward in heaven is great, and I send you there now."

The faun's eyes narrowed as he watched the priest fall slowly earthward in a broadening pool of his own blood.

Father Brennan eased himself to the hard ground and felt the rough hands of the two fauns take a hold and drag him toward the water. The grey sky spread above him, dotted with the bright blue threats of a beautiful day, and he began to feel that perhaps dying wasn't going to be such a bad thing after all. He could feel the coolness of the pond against the back of his neck, and heard his heartbeat slowing in his submerged ears. And then one last thought, the final one he ever had, crossed his mind.

Son of a bitch – it really does feel like slipping into a warm bath.

TWENTY-FOUR

Ezra Schneider rounded the corner from the top of the stairs and walked the fifty feet to the director's office. A girl sat behind a desk chatting happily away on the phone, snapping and chawing on a wad of gum as though it were the last piece of Beeman's on earth.

"I got a page to see the director," Ezra said.

The girl on the phone held up a single digit to indicate she was not particularly interested in why he interrupted her present conversation.

"Naw," she said. "Just waiting for some guy to show up and then I can go."

She couldn't have been more than seventeen or eighteen with mousey brown hair pulled back into a tight bun that awkwardly framed a face slightly too small for the uncomfortably wide head it was firmly stuck to.

"Look, you called me. There are about a million and a half other things I could be enjoying nearly as much as this right now, so if we could just move this along." Ezra barked.

"Wait," she said.

"I have been waiting."

She dismissed him. "Not you, I gotta go, there's some old guy here I need to deal with."

She eyed Ezra as though he were some ancient relic of a man, shuffling around on two antiquated legs that constantly threatened to give out. And here was this fossil, bold as brass, standing in front of her desk, having no other purpose in this life than to annoy the shit out of her at this exact moment.

"May I help you, sir?" The words dripped with so much saccharine insincerity that she nearly choked just saying them.

"Yes," Ezra said sharply. "You can wipe that phoney God-damned smile off of your pudgy God-damned face. That'd be a start."

The young secretary looked for a moment like she might burst into tears, but a sudden spark of resolve flickered and she decided no miserable old man was going to make her cry at twenty minutes to home time on a Friday.

"What can I do for you then?" she said coolly.

"I was paged to the director's office."

"Oh," she said with genuine surprise in her voice. "He must want to see you then."

"Do you assing-well think?"

"He's not here," she said unimpressed.

"What?"

"He left about an hour ago," she explained. "Not a word but see you tomorrow."

"Why in the hell would he page me then?"

"Search me. What is your name?"

"Ezra Schneider."

She pushed out a monstrously large, highly frustrated exhale.

"You might have said that when you first came up here."

"You might have tried harder to get into college and make something of yourself."

"Here." She thrust a fat white envelope at him.

There was a scrap of white paper with his name on it attached to the envelope:

Loyalty is always generously rewarded. You proved your loyalty last night; you've earned this in spades. Good luck with your daughter.

Director.

Ezra dropped the envelope and felt his knees buckle under the sudden feeling of an immense weight placed squarely on his back. Whatever blessed amnesia his brain had afforded to spare him from feeling the truth, slipped away and was crushed under the tidal wave of guilt and loathing over what had occurred less than a day before. A sudden rise of nausea knocked the older man back. He raised an arm to steady himself against the wall.

"I have to go," he said and staggered toward the staircase.

"Oh, hey," she called out to him with sincere concern in her voice. "Hey, don't forget this."

She caught up and pressed the envelope into his hands.

"Yeah, I earned it."

"Are you going to be okay?"

"Just fine. I'm going to hell," he said, and made his way down the stairs.

Ezra walked light-headed past the nurse and her cart full of drugs, bobbed and weaved his way past the seething cauldron of wandering insanity in the main hall, and headed for the front door.

"Ezra Schneider?" a small voice below him said.

"Leave me alone."

He looked around through watery eyes trying desperately to focus on something, anything that might take his mind away from the awful place it was stuck now, and settled on the genial face of the old one, who reached out and took his hand.

"What has happened? There is a blackness around you, like a stain on your soul. Ezra what have you done?"

"None of your God-damned business," he shouted. "Shouldn't you get back to clip-clopping across your bridge? I'm sure the troll misses you."

"You look at me now, Ezra Schneider."

Ezra found it impossible to avoid the elder faun's gaze and stared deep into two amber pools. She began to sing, at first a low and far off sounding rumble of a song, and then, without warning, a high and thin whistle like the whistle of a passing steam train fell on top of it. The lights began to dim and it seemed to Ezra that soon it was just the two of them standing in a darkened room.

The old one released his hand and the lights and sounds of Winterbourne Asylum returned to where they had been.

"I cannot see beyond this wall you have put up around your heart, Ezra Schneider, but you are carrying an awful burden. If you don't unload it soon, you may never be able to."

"I'm not carrying anything."

He looked up at her. She could see the tears well in his eyes and stretched out a hand and rubbed it motherly against his cheek. Ezra closed his eyes for a moment and felt the comfort the faun offered, but the crimson ringed eyes snapped back open and the old man pushed away from her.

"And I'm going to pay for it for the rest of my life."

Ezra pushed past her and out the front door. A blast of November air blew by and what little his stomach held was soon in a pool on the marble landing. The old man took a handkerchief from his back pocket and wiped away the flop sweat that made little, brackish trails into his eyes, and then wiped the remainder of the vomit and coffee from his lower lip. He sucked in as many deep breaths as he could without passing out from light-headedness before making his way down the marble stairs, out onto Parker Street.

The three of them stood before a solid, plaster covered wall in the basement of the asylum.

"No time to waste," the Old One said.

"Oh, right. So, I'll just walk through the wall then?" Redheart asked.

"Do you know nothing of travelling?"

"Of course, you put on the funny clothes, you walk out among the people and they remain calm while you do your shopping," Redheart answered.

"No James, real travelling," she sighed.

A low hum came from deep inside her, a sound that seemed impossible to escape something so small and frail looking. In short order, the hum was accompanied by a high-pitched whistle that defied logic and the walls of Winterbourne began to vibrate. The little faun in the red waistcoat thought the rumbling alone, would bring an onslaught of men in white to make them stop whatever they were doing. It did not. In fact, if Redheart and the others had been able to see what was happening just above them, they would have known that the men in the white uniforms were far too busy with the clanging of the alarm bell and the caterwauling of too many irritable, erratic and generally unhinged people to be interested in anything else. Let alone a rumble that went all but unnoticed.

A small crack appeared on the wall. It spread across the face of it and traveled, vertically at first and then horizontally across the surface. Finally moving vertically downward until a, rectangle shape had been achieved. Redheart moved closer toward and reached out a hand.

"You must open the door, James," the Old One said, the whistling hum ceasing momentarily.

Redheart put his hand against the stone and could feel warmth along it that betrayed what his mind thought it should fee like. He jerked his arm to pull it away from the wall but found it stuck firm.

"I can't let go," he said.

Redheart began to feel the wall pull and tug at him in an undulating pace that gripped and released with increasing and relenting pressure as it moved him inward. Though he couldn't be certain, the little faun was willing bet this is what it felt like being swallowed by a large, cold blooded snake.

"James Redheart, just let go," the elder faun said.

"I can't let go…I can't…I'm…I'm afraid of what's on the other side."

"There's nothing on the other side of the door that you aren't already bringing," she said a smiled at him with a warmth he hadn't felt in ages.

Without much choice, and no opportunity to say anything to either of them, the little faun stopped struggling and resigned himself to whatever lay beyond the reptilian squeeze of the door. Two solid, terrifying squeezes pressed against his chest and legs and he closed his eyes. To his surprise, he hadn't expired but instead, lay on the ground of a forest and could see Karl and the Old One on the other side of the doorway he had just come through.

Karl watched his friend stand and turn slowly in a circle, seemingly getting his bearings and move off toward the west. The little faun turned back to the door just before he disappeared entirely and the barman shot him a forlorn, half-hearted wave. It wasn't returned. Karl felt a dejected sadness as he looked at the elder faun. A satisfied smile bounded its way across her face.

"What are you so happy about?" Karl asked.

"He made it through okay," she answered.

"Was there ever a doubt?"

Oh my, yes. If he'd have kept struggling, the door would've ripped him in two."

Karl suddenly didn't feel well and it showed on his face.

"But it didn't," The Old One said.

"Now what, what do I do?" he asked the old faun.

"You go home. You go back to your bar and you pour your drinks for the nice people in town and you pray your friend makes it out of there in one piece."

"Oh," Karl said quietly.

"I know you want some bigger role to play in all of this but you don't. Your bit in all of this is done but know that you played a most important part in saving both of our worlds Karl, you brought an old faun out of her exile. Go home and wait for your friend. He'll come to you in no time, I know it."

"And you're going to be keeping an eye on all this happening, I assume. Meeting up with your fellow fauns and try to help Redheart from this side?"

"No, not at all. He was totally on his own the second he made it through the door."

"Oh –"

"He'll be fine, Karl. He's a smart kid."

"What are you going to do then?" Karl asked.

"Going back to my room," she answered.

"Going to have a think, figure all of this on your own?"

"No. it's nearly snack time and today is banana pudding. I mental about the stuff."

Without being remotely aware of it, Ezra soon found himself standing in the doorway of Butler's, pacing back and forth and trying to convince himself senses dulled by liquor and piss-poor conversation was infinitely more desirable than what he was currently feeling. He had wandered the town with no real purpose for what seemed like a few minutes to him but was nearer to two hours. He was looking for answers or maybe absolution in the faces of the people who had no idea what an awful person he actually was. When his wandering led him to the grubby bar, he took it as a sign and briefly wrestled with his conscience before he decided to go in. The wearied man wondered whether or not there was enough whisky inside of the establishment to blunt his brain and forget all of the awful things he'd done. He picked a back-corner booth and ordered a glass of top-shelf scotch from the young, gum chewing waitress.

"Was there a sale on gum for twenty something women with no real sense of purpose?" Ezra snapped.

"Huh?" the waitress asked.

"Just bring me the God-damned whisky and gnaw that crap in somebody else's face for a while."

Ezra noticed a large glass jar in front of the liquor shelves half-way full with brine soaked orbs of stomach wrenching torment. He thought for a moment that eating a couple of them and a handful of pretzels might fill the void the coffee had left in its wake. However, a rumble and several gurgles from the basement of his gut assured him that good whisky on an empty stomach was a far better choice than painting the bathroom floor with liquor and bits of pickled eggs.

Karl, the barman, walked up to Ezra's booth with a bottle in his hand and sat down across from him. Ezra eyed the bottle and smiled.

"Twenty-five years old. What do I owe you?" he said.

Karl set down two tumblers, turned the cork from the bottle, and poured a healthy measure of the rich, dark-amber liquid for Ezra and himself.

"My father bought this bottle a long time ago," Karl said, and drained his glass.

Ezra looked up and Karl could see the tears streaming down from crimson flecked eyes. He looked like he hadn't slept in days, his face pale and gaunt, and he'd swear the man's hair looked greyer than it had only a day ago.

"What do you believe happens when you die?" Ezra asked.

"You stop moving and people put you in a nice suit, say nice things about you, and then they eat bundt cake," Karl answered. "Jesus, how much have you had to drink?"

Ezra picked up his glass and raised it in a toast to the barman, drained it in one swallow, and never once took his eyes off of the other man.

"That much? I'm serious. Do you believe in Heaven and Hell, eternal damnation and all that?" Ezra asked.

"I don't know that I believe in angels and devils," Karl answered. "I've recently met a couple of devils I'd trust with my life, and I've known a few angels whose ears I wouldn't piss in if their brains were on fire."

He stared into the distance for a short time and raised a hand out in front of him as though he plucked his next thought from thin air like he might take a ripe apple from a tree.

"I would like to think, I hope, that there is at least justice."

"Justice?" Ezra asked.

"Justice. The wicked get their punishment, maybe not right away or even when it would do any good, but I always hope that the world finds some way of putting things right in the end."

"What about someone who did something wrong? Something awful, though they thought it was for the right reasons?" Ezra asked.

"I don't know that it makes a difference. My mother used to say, if you run over somebody by accident or if you run over them on purpose, they're still run over."

Ezra pushed the bottle toward Karl and stood to leave.

"Thanks for the drink, Karl."

"Take it. Go home, get drunk with your wife."

"My wife left."

"I'm sorry. I didn't..."

"She went three weeks after Isobel disappeared. Went to her sister's in Peoria."

"Oh," Karl said. "How are you getting on?"

"She wasn't much of a wife anyway," Ezra chuckled.

He blotted his eyes with a handkerchief and then trumpeted loud, nasal burst before replacing it in his pocket.

"Good thing you didn't do that the other way around," Karl joked.

Ezra managed a pained, half smile and stepped out into the early evening. He pulled the stopper on the bottle as the door of Butler's closed behind him and stepped onto the street after a healthy swig.

A figure stood on the walk opposite him, a woman who, although she seemed desperately familiar to him, he couldn't quite place. There was something about her face, something wrong and slightly inhuman – like looking at a photograph through warped glass. He took another pull off the bottle and she was gone. By the time he hit Millar's field, little more than a third of the bottle and slightly less than a third of his sobriety remained.

Ezra arrived at home and pushed open the door that hadn't been locked since his wife had gone. He switched on the kitchen light that flickered on and off ceaselessly in the dying spiral of cheap fluorescent lighting and rummaged around in drawers and cupboards, pulling on the bottle all the while. When he finally found what he searched for, the white-haired man stumbled into the sitting room, took a small picture down from the mantle, and removed the image of his daughter from the frame.

Schneider took another long pull from the fine, expensive whisky and realized he was no longer alone. Ezra recognized the figure from across the street at Butler's and, now seeing clearly who it was, the old man he guessed she'd been with him since leaving Winterbourne Asylum. She was slightly heavy set with dark hair and eyes as lifeless and blanched as they had been in that terrible room. The figure wasn't menacing him, nor was she pointing and shouting at him accusingly. But neither was she going away.

"Would it matter if I said I was sorry?" he pleaded to the lifeless eyes.

She offered no reply, nor did she offer him any forgiveness. But neither did she leave.

Ezra reached into his pocket and produced the small black and white photo of Isobel and held it up for the figure to see. He groped around in his brain for the words that might assuage her, might make the ghastly figure understand it wasn't about him or greed, it was always about the girl in the photograph. The dark-haired woman continued to stare through the whites of her eyes, never moving their passionless gaze from Ezra's face.

The old man rose quickly and made a stumbling run for the back bedroom, the room meant for the second child that never came. It was now the bed he slept in if he'd had too much to drink, or if the atmosphere in the marriage bed was just too icy. He slept in this room more often than not.

Ezra opened the small closet on the back wall and took down a dust covered, Florsheim shoe box and tucked it under his arm. As the closet door closed, he saw her emerge from behind it, white eyes still staring, expression fixed and blank. Never changing, never flinching, and never leaving.

Ezra took the lid off the shoe box and stared at the nickel-plated revolver inside it, his thoughts twisting images of a terrified dark-haired woman and a frightened little girl around in his head and boiling over until, without much thought about it, he took the cold steel in hand and raised it up to mouth level. The pale-haired man thought for a moment he could detect a faint smile playing across the pale lips of the cadaverous woman, but when he cocked the hammer back, it was replaced by a look of genuine fear.

"Why Dada?" He could hear Isobel, almost see her walking toward him from the endless flickering light of the kitchen. "Why did you hurt that woman, Dada?"

The pale woman stood staring. Ezra watched a single tear roll away from one of her ghastly pale eyes. Without warning, she was gone. He put the gleaming barrel between his teeth, screamed in defiance of all of his fears and squeezed the trigger.

TWENTY-FIVE

The priest's body floated gently on the small pond, bobbing and rocking in the light breeze, looking more like a contented, summer bather than the corpse of a disgraceful cleric. And if it weren't for the truth of it all, the whole scene might have looked entirely idyllic.

"Isn't something supposed to happen?" Dreadhorn asked.

"I don't know." Lucerne sounded slightly disappointed.

"What do you mean you don't know?"

"I mean I do not know, right? It's not as though there's a guide book for all of this. Oh wait, there is."

He skimmed quickly through the large book Dreadhorn retrieved earlier and came to a group of three illustrations of the fountain and pond. Two small fauns stood in front with a body surrounded by crimson floating in the water's centre. Next to the first image seemed to be the depiction of an explosion or perhaps a large spout of water where the body had been. Two small fauns stood on the shore. The final image unveiled a huge, faun-like creature standing next to the body of one small faun and long squiggles of lines coming from the pond.

"Those pictures look quite specific, don't you think?" Dreadhorn asked.

"I suppose, but what possible difference should that make?" the king of all fauns responded.

"None to whomever is not the faun laying on the ground beneath that thing."

"I suppose something is meant to happen around our dearly departed friend. Wouldn't you agree Maurice?" Lucerne said.

As if on cue, the water below the priest's floating remains began to churn and roil, and he drifted toward the edge of the pond. A thin black tendril shot up from below the water, quickly wrapping itself around the inert priest's ankle. It pulled him toward the centre of the pond.

"Something like that?" Dreadhorn asked.

"Tell me, Maurice, what is that feeling you get when strange things suddenly seem very dangerous, perhaps evening life threatening?" Lucerne said.

"Um," Dreadhorn said, not entirely understanding the question. "Fear, sir?"

Lucerne sighed. "Yes, that's it. I am feeling very strongly that we should flee this place in a heated rush, but it would seem an immeasurable amount of fear is coursing through me and I'm rather paralyzed by the stuff."

Dreadhorn looked at the king and a wicked thought floated through his head. He could just leave. The thick faun wasn't paralyzed by fear, or anything else for that matter, and if staying around to see what pulled the priest's body to the bottom of the pond didn't seem like a good idea, he felt he was within his rights to just bugger off. Sergeant at arms and high protector, so far as he was concerned, did not extend into the realms of the otherworldly.

Lucerne could see it now, long and black and covered in the primordial ooze that lay on the bottom of the pond. It resembled an arm, growing thicker toward the water but tapering slightly at the end to a small, digit-like appendage that undulated toward the bobbing, lifeless body of the priest. The tendril coiled around the priest's torso like a serpent constricting the last breath out of its prey. In a split second, the late Father Winslow Brennan disappeared under a rush of frothing water.

"Now what?" Lucerne asked.

A great plume of crimson, sanguineous water shot from the pond and fell back into it, then rose and fell again only slightly higher, and rose and fell a third time, only to fall deathly silent and still again. Dreadhorn stepped back as the water began to churn and a large, foaming mass launched itself toward the shore where the king of all fauns stood.

"I think we'd better–" the king began.

A black tendril, three times as long as Lucerne had seen wrap around the priest, shot from the water, and wrapped itself around his throat. It pulled him into the water. He struggled against it, trying to inch farther back up the shore, but it only forced the whip-like thing to tighten. Dropping to his knees, the king of all fauns reached out a desperate, panicked arm to Dreadhorn who stood along the shore.

Stunned by what he saw, unable to move to help his king and unsure if he really wanted to, the sergeant at arms glanced at his master once more and quickly moved away from the pond. A look of fear and betrayal flashed on Lucerne's face and after that, it was a matter of minutes before the king of all fauns exhausted his strength and was dragged quietly beneath the water.

The surviving faun thought, if he were to remain the surviving faun, leaving in fairly short order should be first on the list of things to do in the dawn of this new era. But as he turned to leave, a long black whip shot from the water and held him firmly where he stood. Dreadhorn pulled back against it instinctively but got no farther away from the pond. Fearing the worst, he reached for the small black handled knife but found it missing from its usual home. He'd given it to the king who, in his kingly wisdom, had not given it back, and now he found himself groping hopefully at his waist while the black tendril continued to restrict all movement.

The faun's mind raced as he scanned the area around the pond for something to remove the black serpentine thing. Dreadhorn suddenly became aware it wasn't pulling him anywhere, so much as it just wasn't letting him leave.

"Have something important to show me, have we?"

The tentacle tightened slightly and slackened again.

"Need me to stay here, do we?"

Another gentle tightening and slackening.

"Oh, very well," Dreadhorn sighed.

The ooze covered tendril released its grip and slunk back under the water.

"I could just run you know," Dreadhorn shouted at the retreating thing.

The tentacle shot back at him like the crack of a whip, faster than it had moved before and much faster than the faun thought it could. The black slime-covered tendril formed itself up and around in a shape like a gibbet and dropped an offshoot in the shape of a noose just above his face.

"Ah yes," the faun gulped. "Yes, there is that."

The black, vine-like thing coiled itself around him several times, first at his waist and arms and then finally around his throat. Giving gentle squeezes to all the bits, letting the faun know it wasn't going to let him go anywhere anytime soon, and if it so desired, the slimy tendril could pop his eyes out of their sockets with one good squeeze. When it seemed satisfied he wasn't leaving, the muck-covered thing slunk away and disappeared beneath the water again.

The bubbling of the water rose to a fever-pitch and then, all at once, ceased entirely. The pond went deathly still. A thin line appeared directly down the centre, stretching from end to end. The water began to recede away from the line like two great curtains being drawn across a window, and a lone figure stood in the now exposed foulness at the bottom of the pond.

Dreadhorn could see the figure was vaguely faun shaped, and heading directly toward him at a pace that suggested he hadn't a care in the world. With the water gone, he could see the bottom of the pond sloped upward, and in no time, Dreadhorn and the other faun faced each other on the bank.

The faun, who Dreadhorn guessed was roughly his size at a distance, now moved into clear view and he could see that this fellow was larger than him, easily a whole head and shoulders and a generous portion of his very muscular back taller. He was glorious, the very epitome of faundom. Well-muscled legs covered in thick, well-groomed chestnut hair atop glistening black hooves. His torso rose long and tall and golden, bronzed skin barely covered the muscles beneath it. The faun's thin featured face appeared too delicate, with a proud nose and soft amber eyes.

A full chestnut-coloured beard framed the face giving him an altogether regal appearance. From the top of his head stretched an immense, majestic rack of stag horns that only served to reinforce his noble visage. Were it not for a certain ferocity, he could sense beneath the taller faun's calm exterior, Dreadhorn would have thought him too pretty to be of much use for anything apart from standing on a pedestal somewhere and looking good.

Dreadhorn didn't know this impressive faun, but he was fairly certain he didn't much care for him. In fact, he may have hated him.

"And you would be?" Dreadhorn asked.

"Your superior in every way," the handsome faun said.

His voice deepened and the whole forest seemed to shake under the enormity of the sound.

"And who might you be?"

"I, ahem… I am Maurice Chevalier Dreadhorn." Dreadhorn's voice made a slight crack as he spoke to the golden faun.

"No doubt one of the fauns of Na Doireachan?"

"The same."

"Excellent. I have need of assistance, I'm sure you will prove adequate."

"Adequate. I am sergeant at arms and high protector to his majesty Lucerne III king of all fauns."

"Whose remains are currently being picked over and sinking into the filth and mire of this pond."

"Yes, well," Dreadhorn sputtered.

"Not much in the way of protection, are we? Anything else, anything to add to your glorious title?" the handsome faun said, mocking.

"Isn't it enough? Who are you to insult me?" Dreadhorn spat.

He reached again for the black handled knife that still wasn't in his belt and imagined what he would do had it been there.

"Who am I to insult you? I am the mountain top boy. I am the golden sun, majestic in an azure sky. I am the first light at the dawn of time and I am the last glowing ember at the end of days," he said

"Oh yes. Do you have that written down someplace?" Dreadhorn fumbled for a pithy comeback.

The taller faun's eyes narrowed with anger and he leaned into Dreadhorn's face, snorting in derision. He snapped his fingers and a dozen black tendrils erupted from the pond, seizing the smaller faun around the arms and legs. The high protector jerked forcefully upward and remained hanging slightly above the ground, face to face with the golden faun.

"I, dullard, am Urisk. First of my kind, and I look down on you because there are none higher. If you will not aid me, I will find one who will."

"And what will happen to me if I refuse?"

"I will visit ruination upon you, to your very soul, and my pet will suck the marrow from the splinters of your shattered bones."

Dreadhorn could feel the electric excitement coursing through the tentacles as they tightened their grip.

"Command me, my lord," the faun said.

TWENTY-SIX

Isobel sat next to the small bonfire Redheart had built to warm them. The sun crept slowly beneath the horizon. The occasionally warm November days now gave way to seasonally crisp nights. She closed her eyes and smiled at the warmth of the rising flames.

The three mice suddenly began to race around frantically, snapping at one another and scraping the sides of their heads along the ground as though some unseen hand twisted their necks in amusement.

"What. What's the matter?" Isobel shrieked.

Isobel heard the voice in her head but it no longer sounded calm and soothing. Genuine fear warped and distorted it into something high-pitched and grating – a voice desperate to organize itself and the thoughts of three very frightened mice.

"Late. Too late, too late," they squeaked.

"What's too late? Too late for what?" Isobel said.

"Too late, can't stop it now!"

"Do you know what she's talking about?" Isobel asked, turning to Redheart.

"I could ask I suppose."

Redheart pushed himself up and moved in the direction the mice seemed to be scurrying the most.

"What exactly are you talking about?" the faun asked particularly loudly.

"I could have done that."

"Then why didn't you?" Redheart asked, completely misunderstanding the sarcasm in her voice.

She grabbed an old corn broom from beside the door of the wooden shack and put the blanket that covered the doorway on the ground in as comfortable a heap as possible. Isobel shooed the three mice onto the blanket. When she was satisfied they were going to stay on it, she picked it up and cradled the three of them in her arms.

"Shhh. Now tell me, what's happened. What's too late?" she soothed.

The voice in her head seemed like it took a deep breath, and then another. After several more, it spoke.

"I had hoped that with you here, the transformation wouldn't have taken place and we might have a bit more time."

"Transformation? More time?" Isobel asked.

"The black sun has begun its journey. A blood moon will rise tonight. "Urisk has awoken," the voice said.

"What?" Redheart gasped. "But she's here. Isobel is here. How is this possible?"

"Lucerne must have found another human to sacrifice."

"Sacrifice? Lucerne was going to kill me?"

"Do try to keep up. Isn't much of a blood moon without blood, is it?" the voice in her head said.

Isobel looked slowly around the cabin before heading for the hanging blanket door.

"Where are you going?" Redheart asked.

"I've just found out that everything I believed I came here for is a complete lie. I would like very much to go home, and I'm pretty sure that if I start walking now, I can be there in time for breakfast."

"But we need you," the voice said.

Isobel looked at the three twitching noses and the three sets of gleaming black eyes staring up at her and thought, for a second, she might set the blanket down and say bugger to the whole thing.

"Need what? I'm guessing there isn't a problem with the water supply in the village?" Isobel asked.

"A model of efficiency!" Redheart beamed.

"Right. And you need me for what, then?"

"Lucerne, has taken the powers of Urisk, the first of our kind, and now all will surely…"

"That's not entirely true. Lucerne is dead and gone by now I should think," the voice said.

"But the prophecy, the stories of old?" Redheart questioned.

"All lies," the voice said.

"But I—"

"Look, all power comes at a price, and the power to come back from where he was is very expensive. Urisk knew that no faun would have a problem taking the life of a human if it meant unlimited power, so he left out the bit about his returning and needing the blood of a faun to do so when he wrote it all down."

"Wait what? Urisk wrote the prophecies about him… himself?" Redheart stammered.

"Oh sure. Most of the best ones are written by the ones they're about. Why do you think the subjects all come out so well, all rising from the grave and fat ear lobes laughing into the abyss and such?" the voice said.

Why would he do it?" Redheart wondered.

"Look around you. Urisk the magnificent, Urisk the stupendous, Urisk the bloody well above ordinary. Who would want that to end?" the voice answered.

"I'm not following," Redheart said.

"When Urisk first appeared, the humans loved him, made him a star of stage and circus tent everywhere he went. But tastes change and humans are a fickle lot. Soon they were on to another living homage to the bizarre and the devil from the mountains was cast aside with the refuse."

"But what about the first men? What about driving him out with whips and piercing his side with wicked spears?" the faun protested.

"All dime novel rubbish. No one drove him out except in a carriage to the next town over. Urisk came out here because no one wanted him anymore."

Redheart stood silently, letting the words sink in.

"Hello?" Isobel said.

"Yes?" the voice answered.

"This is all very interesting, and I am enjoying learning all about you and your stories, but I'm failing to see what any of it has to do with me. Now either one of you explains it to me or I *am* going home."

"The thing is, a short while ago, it had very little to do with you. You were a bit of an insurance against things going sour. I was certain you were the only human wandering about Na Doireachan, so it was just a matter of training you up a bit and sending you on your way," the voice said.

Isobel shook her head, confused by all of it.

"So, this fellow found somebody else? And now he is resurrected? I still don't see–"

"That's the bit I'm fuzzy on too, so what if he came back? Yes, it's rather stupendous and considerably above average, but what difference does it make if he cheated death and came back?" Redheart interrupted.

"Because he isn't cheating death. Mostly because he can't actually die," the voice said.

"How's that?" Redheart said.

"Not everything he wrote was a lie. Urisk appeared out of nowhere, that much is true, and once he left the world of men he came here. This is also the truth. Here he met with a female like himself and they created the fauns of Na Doireachan. What those stories don't tell you and, this is how you can tell they were bloody well written by him and perpetuated by more like him, was that she showed him the power that was inside of him. He had no idea up to then. Males, they're all the same, aren't they?"

"I'm still not quite understanding all of this." Isobel became flustered and a little embarrassed at her inability to see where this was all heading.

The voice sighed. "Oh dear. Enjoying your time at the kiddies table, are you? Not quite ready to sit with Mummy and Daddy and use a sharp knife?"

Isobel's face flushed in minor humiliation.

"Urisk developed an intense hatred for your kind, swore vengeance on them for forsaking him. Once the power within him had been discovered, he set about getting revenge for the insult the humans had offered. If the humans of Winterbourne wouldn't celebrate his majesty, they would cower before his wrath."

"What is he?" Isobel asked, suddenly feeling like she was part of the conversation.

"I don't know that there is a name for it. Eternal, elemental, wielder of fire and all powerful, they all apply," the voice said.

"But you're the female, doesn't that count for something?" Isobel asked, feeling a little less than clever that she hadn't caught onto it before now.

"What do you mean?"

"I mean aren't you the opposite of him? If he is all evil, doesn't that make you all good?"

"I'm not sure I follow you."

"You're the spirit of the other faun or whatever you are, aren't you? So, if he is the fire you must be the opposite, right?"

The three mice curled up in the blanket and managed to come as close as mice could come to blushing.

"Yes. If Urisk is the flame, I am the water."

"And I'm guessing you already know what happens with fire and water," Isobel said, almost to herself and a smile crept its way across her face.

TWENTY-SEVEN

"After we put Urisk underneath the fountain…" the voice inside Isobel's head said.

"Wait. What shall I call you? Mice seems a little informal," Isobel said.

"Ah yes. There were some that called me The Cailleach, the hag," the voice said.

"Oh?"

"Leaves a little to be desired, I know."

"Maybe if I called you mouse, rather than mice?" Isobel said trying to be helpful.

"I recall the name May. I think Urisk called me May," she said, barely above a whisper.

"What?" Redheart asked.

"You're not sure?" Isobel asked.

"I have been called so many things by so many people and I have been as I am now for some time. Memories blur together and fade to darkness. I remember the name but I cannot say for certain it was mine."

"I think it's a lovely name. Much better than calling you a hag," Isobel said.

"*The* Hag."

Isobel looked at the three mice trying to decide whether the name suited them. She figured it was as good a name as any, and before she could say anything to that effect, May continued with her story.

"After we put Urisk underneath the fountain," May repeated.

"Wait, we? There was someone else there?" Redheart asked.

"Our first born. As clever as her mother and as powerful as both of us. It was really she that did all the work, I just moved around stumps and arranged the bushes and what not."

The three mice rose up from the blanket and made their way quickly up Isobel's bathrobe, settling at her shoulder.

"Right then." May and three sets of black eyes trained themselves on Isobel. "Shall we begin?"

"Begin what?" Isobel asked.

"The transfer of course. I'm going to take all of my essence from these mice and put it into you."

"What?" Isobel asked.

"Yes, my dear. You'll never put him back under the fountain otherwise," May said.

"I'm not putting anybody anywhere!"

"Nonsense, there has only been one other like you, and I should think she would be much too old for this sort of thing," May said.

"Like me?" Isobel asked.

"A true child of nature," Redheart said gravely.

"Yes, nothing else to add to that?" Isobel asked.

"Well it's just…" the faun fumbled.

"Why is every little thing in this place accompanied by so much mystery? Couldn't we just get right to the point without all the heavy breathing and gnashing of teeth?"

"She has got a point, James," the hag said.

"Oh, very well. You possess the power to control the four elements. Like your predecessor, you have the abilities of both The Cailleach and Urisk. Only slightly lesser," Redheart said.

"Slightly lesser?"

"Sounds better than watered down," the faun answered.

"I will give you the abilities you will need. From me you will learn to call the void, you will never confine him without it. Now, just you open up and let the three mice wee in your mouth," May said.

"What?" Isobel said, aghast at the thought.

"Still paying attention then." May laughed. "Very good. Now if you let each one of my three friends here touch your lips."

Isobel remained cautiously still as the first of the mice touched its lips to hers. As it ran down her arm she suddenly began to feel full, as though she had just eaten a large Sunday dinner.

"Oh, I wasn't expecting that."

"Two more. Won't be long now," May said.

The second mouse moved into place and she soon felt like she imagined her father did after Christmas dinner.

"That's good, that's enough now. I don't think I can do anymore," Isobel said.

"You must, my dear. It's nearly finished," the hag said.

"I can't. It's too much."

"James, if you would," she said.

Redheart moved to Isobel and reluctantly grabbed her by the shoulders, holding her in place.

"No. Really, I can't."

"No." Redheart held her tighter, to the point where her arms ached. "Really, you must!"

The faun pushed her down to her knees, then on to her back, and the final mouse touched its small, thin lips to hers. Isobel felt a surge of something vast and immeasurably strong course through her. She didn't feel full anymore, like she had eaten everything that had ever existed. Now, she felt impossibly strong – like she could pull down the pillars of the earth, stone by mountainous stone, and carry them home in her pocket.

The girl stood slowly and her gaze darted around the room, taking everything in, finally coming to rest on Redheart.

"How do you feel?" the faun asked.

"Overwhelming."

The three mice looked up from her feet and May's voice echoed in her ears.

"I have poured all of my knowledge into you. All that I am, all that I was ever capable of, now resides in you. My journey is now at an end," the voice said.

"What do you mean at an end? Like retirement at an end, like you get to go somewhere warm for a while, at an end?" Isobel asked.

"I suppose that depends on what type of life I've led. I told you before that all power comes at a price. There wasn't very much left of me after the last time we imprisoned Urisk. There is nothing left of me now that isn't inside of you," May said.

"But that isn't fair," Isobel shouted, and the trees all around the makeshift cabin seemed to bend and move away from the force of her voice. The girl looked around, unsure if she had caused the trees to move in a, seemingly, fearful manner and a little embarrassed when it looked to be true.

"No, it isn't, but then neither is life. You just get used to it," the hag's soft voice said.

"What if I say no, what if I give it all back to you?"

"Then there'll be no one to stop him. And he will burn Winterbourne and every living thing in it to cinders," May answered.

The three mice looked up from her feet and suddenly realized they were three very small mice in a very large and unsafe world. Without much more thought, they scurried away from Isobel and the ramshackle cabin. And, with their departure, the voice inside Isobel's head, the voice of the Cailleach, the mother of the forest, was silent.

Isobel felt the burning sting of tears rise and walked outside, hurrying a few feet from the cabin until she found what looked like a suitable tree and sat down. The dried leaves and heaps of pine needles were surprisingly more comfortable than they looked. Cautiously she called out to the quiet of the forest, and when it appeared no one had followed her, she fell apart.

The blonde girl wept and wept until her body shook so much she feared it might not stop, and went on, well past the point of tears and into silent keening. Isobel wept for her town and the people she didn't know, and likely never would. Wept at the thought of it as a smoking ruin full of aimless, wandering husks of men and women looking for children they wouldn't find. Then, after a time, the tears returned. A little bit anyway, for her mother and father too. A father who would never know what she'd found beyond the veil of black flies, inside this wondrous emerald world.

"Would you like something to drink?" Redheart asked.

"What?"

"As a kid, my mother told me that when you lot get upset, you like to have a beverage. So I was asking you if you'd like something to drink."

"Do you have a beverage?"

"All I have is a skin full of Banewort brandy."

"All right."

She took the skin from the faun and hoisted it to her lips. It tasted like a slap across the face.

"Ugh!" Isobel sputtered. "What's in that?"

The juice of the Banewort plant fermented and distilled in our village."

"It's like lighter fluid."

Redheart took a long pull on the bag and put the cork firmly back in the neck of the skin. He wasn't certain what lighter fluid was, but if it tasted half as good as this fine brandy, he would be willing to give it a go as soon as he could.

Isobel admired the faun sitting with a satisfied look on his face, reasoning it may have been his nature to find a kind of balance in all situations or that his head might be swimming a bit from the brandy.

"What should I do?" she asked after a while.

"What does your heart tell you?"

"My heart tells me that two days ago I was just the weird girl who sat at the back of the room. Nobody liked me, and most of them were a little afraid of me. How can I possibly be this saviour?"

"You won't be," the faun said.

"What do you mean?" Isobel asked, a little stunned by the statement.

"You won't be a saviour, you will continue to be the weird girl at the back of the room if you go back or if you stay and help. No one will know about what you do either way. Funny thing about you lot, you only believe what you want to believe, even if you see evidence to the contrary. No one will know about you because no one cares."

"Then why do it?"

"Because it's the right thing to do."

TWENTY-EIGHT

The first traces of the rising sun oozed and bleed their way along the horizon, slow and viscous like coral-coloured honey. Ezra opened his eyes to a very different world, a world where he couldn't discern any colour. As though a great wound had opened in the centre of the room and all the taupe and burnt umber and dusty rose that his wife had so loved, gushed out and left a blanched husk behind.

His head pounded, and though he hadn't actually moved his hands around it, he was fairly certain it was still attached to his neck. Raising an arm and groping the air slowly, the old man found the handle to the closet door and used it to pull himself up from the floor.

Half awake and even less clear-headed, Ezra inched his way around the small bedroom until he was certain he could make it more than a couple of steps without tipping over. As the old man moved back toward the closet door, he saw the nickel-plated revolver laying on a large stain on the cheap grey carpet. Thinking for a moment, his hand moved for it but something deep down said whatever he was likely to encounter, he wouldn't need it.

The white-haired man walked slowly into the kitchen and smiled as he spied the whisky bottle that contained more of the amber liquid than he recalled leaving. He poured a glass, feeling suddenly too embarrassed to keep draining it by lifting the bottle to his mouth like some old wino. After quickly emptying the first glass and pouring himself another, he walked into the bathroom.

The light fixture above the bathroom sink gave a loud electric hum followed by a firecracker pop that left Ezra in half-light, staring at the mirror. The old man raised a hand to his face and couldn't feel any wound after running three fingers along one cheek and on to the other side. Nor any after moving a hand over the back of his head. The reflection in the mirror, however, painted an altogether different picture.

A horrid and unnatural mottling darkened the corners of his mouth, trailing down to the chin like the residue from thick, black, acrid smoke being suddenly blown at his face. A jagged hole opened near the bottom of his right jaw, large enough to see the inside of his mouth and the broken shards of the few teeth that still remained. Above the gaping opening in the jaw, his eye, or what was left of it, stared blankly downward as it dangled precariously from the socket. Ezra ran the flat of his right hand along his face and marvelled at feeling none of the gore or caked-on blood that stared back at him from the mirror. The white-haired man raised the whisky glass in salute of the broken face looking at him.

"To your very good health," Ezra said.

"Thank-you," the image answered and the whisky glass smashed on the floor.

Ezra turned from the mirror, frantic to escape the awful image in it, only to find it standing behind him staring at the remains of the shattered glass on the floor.

"Oh dear. Nothing worse than a waste of good whisky," he sighed.

"Okay, oh dear, is something old ladies say after they fart during church. So, if you aren't me, who the hell are you?"

"That's not so easy to explain," the man said.

"Try me."

The next second Ezra pulled a Chesterfield from the pocket of his shirt and, after sparking it to life, took a long, thoughtful drag. He then exhaled the smoke above his head. As he lowered his head, the hideous wounds began to fade and soon, two identical Ezra's stood face to face.

"You might say I'm a messenger," second Ezra said.

"Messenger?"

"There's a beginning and an end to all things – time, space, life, games of horseshoe, you get the idea. Everything that starts must also end. I am a servant of the ultimate end."

"What do you want with me?" Ezra asked.

"You might have noticed that you're currently *not* resting in peace, despite having just eaten a bullet."

"I was wondering about that."

"You're a unique case. You've broken two of the big rules. The two biggest, really."

"And this is hell I suppose."

"No. This is your bathroom. The décor in hell is much worse. That's my point. You took a life and then you took your own," second Ezra said.

"Surely, I'm not the first person to ever do that?"

"No, not even the first one today."

"Then what's the problem?"

"You are the first person to take two lives as a completely selfless act, both times. You did something so very, very wrong but for all the right reasons."

Ezra grew silent and lowered his head.

"Are you here to take me… away?"

"No. It was decided that since your situation is unique, your punishment must be equally so."

"I don't like the sounds of that," Ezra said.

"You're not going to like the rest of it either. Let's go sit down and have a glass of that scotch. It's been a while since I've tasted anything as good as that."

The two Ezra Schneiders left the bathroom and headed down the narrow hallway toward a modest sitting room, stopping by the kitchen to grab the bottle and two nearly clean glasses. They sat sharing drinks in silence until the not-Ezra Schneider at last broke the quiet tension by clearing his throat. He downed the rest of the whisky, slowly and deliberately and stood to face Ezra.

"I have good news and bad news," he said.

"Does it matter which one I hear first?"

"Not particularly."

"Fire away."

"Your daughter is alive and well. And you are going to live forever or very nearly to it."

Ezra Schneider felt the tears well-up and turned away from his double for fear this was all a dream and, after waking, he didn't want to remember his subconscious self as a blubbering wreck.

"That doesn't sound like much of a punishment. I don't get it," Ezra said.

"Your daughter will spend the rest of her life believing that you took your own life last night, though she will never know or understand the reasons why. You will never speak to her or have contact with her again. I suspect she will place the blame squarely on herself," the twin said

"Wait, what. But that's not fair!"

The other Ezra's face flickered as though a light bulb somewhere behind his skin was going through the agonizing final throes of its life. He seemed to grow in height and his face vanished, replaced with a shape similar to a face but with the appearance of shimmering, liquid metal.

"You took the life of another, and long before its time was up. Fair would be your flayed corpse, wearing honey underpants atop an ant mound. There were many who wanted far worse for you," the faceless man said.

A wave of shame and revulsion rose from deep in Ezra's stomach, and the hot creeping sweat of fear beaded and prickled his forehead. He fired the rest of the scotch down and poured himself another generous glass. Staring mindlessly at the golden liquid in the glass, the ashen-faced man stood and moved to the small window at the back of the sitting room.

Isobel's father downed his whisky and stared out the window at the yellowing grass of his front lawn. The irony wasn't lost on him that his grass was dead and now, for all intents and purposes, so was he.

"It had to be like this," the mirror faced man said.

"I would've liked to have said good-bye."

TWENTY-NINE

"Might be a good idea to give it a bit of a go. You've been down there awhile," Dreadhorn said.

"Do you doubt my abilities?" Urisk demanded.

"No, I doubt your accuracy after laying dormant for so long. Go on, let's see something."

The taller faun stood at the edge of the pond and raised a hand, palm up, motioning toward the water as though he were asking it to come to him. The pond bubbled and looked for the right moment to obey the gesture, but it came and went without much bother, and the froth soon fizzled and the water fell smooth and calm again.

"Ah, you see?"

Urisk glared and waved the smaller faun off.

He tried again with similar results, and sat down on the bank of the pond.

He sighed. "I'm cold. Get a fire a going."

"Ah well… The thing is… ah you see it's…"

"Are you not capable of summoning fire?"

"Capable? Yes. Skilfully capable? Not entirely," Dreadhorn said.

Urisk shot the other faun a look that explained dire consequences were imminent if a fire was not produced, and quickly at that. After several laughable attempts, Dreadhorn managed to flake off a few sparking bits and produced a suitably impressive pile of smouldering moss.

"Give it a blow," Urisk said.

Dreadhorn let loose a series of short, puffy breaths and succeeded in creating a ghastly amount of thick, grey smoke. Anyone within a hundred miles of them with the wherewithal to read smoke signals, would have immediately gotten the message that said, "Hello, we are freezing to death and now we can't see anything."

"At the bottom," Urisk said.

"What?" Dreadhorn snapped.

"Blow at the bottom. Long, steady breaths."

The faun did as he was told and, after three very patient breaths, a small flame began to tease its way in and out of the pile of smoking flora.

"Hey!" Dreadhorn exclaimed.

"Truly a wonder to behold," Urisk chided.

The two fauns sat warming themselves by the fire in overwhelming silence for what seemed to Dreadhorn to be far too long a time.

"What's our next step? Or rather our first step?"

"I have been under that fountain nearly longer than I can remember. One thing, one singular thought, kept me focused enough and gave me the will to endure close to a century of captivity."

"Fresh fields, thick with new, green hay. The cool, fresh waters of the Nyegard, chewing on a wonderful old tin can," Dreadhorn said.

"What? No, not that at all. Revenge. Revenge against those who cast me out and those who put me under the fountain."

Urisk stretched out his hands to the warmth of the fire and felt the heat bend toward him, enveloping him to his elbows. As he turned his hands from palm up to palm down and back again, the flames began to dance in rhythm with them. The faun twirled his finger slightly and a small cyclone of flame appeared before him, spinning faster with each revolution his finger made.

The golden faun grinned an awful, beastly, grin, and stood, closing his hand into a fist. As he did, the small vortex collapsed into an even smaller ball of flame, pulsating, undulating, and glowing as it hung above the burning logs of the fire. He opened his hand and saw the flame ball widen and flatten to take on the appearance of a small bird. As he moved his hands, the bird followed suit and flapped side to side leaving glowing streaks of chimney-red and Halloween-orange light in its wake.

Urisk brought up his hands, first one and then the other, and the avian flame stopped dead in front of him, motionless, and seeming to wait for his next command. He slowly widened the space between his palms and the bird grew larger. The heat that poured off of it, became nearly unbearable. As he tilted his hands up, the huge incendiary thing took off in a shower of apricot sparks and plumes of pearly smoke toward the tops of the trees. In minutes, the branches were engulfed in flame and the fire bird turned, baring down on Dreadhorn.

"Please sir, no!" the smaller faun begged.

The larger faun allowed Dreadhorn to feel the full heat of the giant ethereal flame before clapping his hands together and watching the bird disappear, raining smoke and embers down on the faun.

Dreadhorn motioned to the burning treetops and remarked, "If left unchecked sir, those could prove catastrophic to all fauns in this glade."

Urisk turned his gaze toward the water, and after a few innocuous hand gestures, a large roiling span of water rose up, unsteadily, from the pond. As he raised his hands, the large, floating puddle moved slowly upward and began to mingle with the burning foliage. In short order, they were reduced to a soggy lot of steaming, leafless tree tops.

"We make for Winterbourne. The humans will know fear this day," the golden faun said.

"Excellent choice sir."

"I have a small cabin not far from here. We will take some nourishment there and move on to the town in the morning."

"So, the humans will know fear tomorrow?" Dreadhorn said.

THIRTY

"Give it a go," Redheart coaxed.

"Give what a go?" Isobel asked.

"You know, the stuff." Redheart thrust both arms forward with grave determination and wiggled his fingers dramatically.

"What? Play the piano?"

"Don't be thick. You know what I'm talking about."

She stared at him for a moment with a puzzled look on her face.

"What is it?" the faun asked.

"I'm a little nervous. I can feel it in there, all of it... all of her. She's inside my head. It's like a headache big enough to split the world, like a giant pressure behind my eyes that feels like it, if I give it half a chance, may explode out the top of my head."

"The Cailleach wouldn't have given this to you if she didn't think you were capable of handling it."

"Do you suppose I should wiggle my fingers?" Isobel giggled.

The girl imitated his gesture as the words left her and hundreds of the tiniest, prettiest red and blue flowers erupted from the ground below her. A smile made its way across her mouth and she felt, suddenly, beautiful and powerful.

"Exceptionally mediocre. But hardly what I would call offensive. Try something else," Redheart urged.

Isobel closed her eyes and tried to concentrate on something, anything really. The merciless doubt crept through her mind and whispered things she nearly thought anyway, things she already knew. That Isobel Schneider was not anybody's chosen one or the true child of nature, and nothing special – certainly nothing to be feared. She opened her eyes and saw Redheart standing in front of her, disappointment rising in his expression.

"I can't."

"If you quiet your mind you will hear it," said the voice in her head.

"Hear what?" the girl asked.

"My gift," the woman's voice answered.

The girl closed her eyes again, and after too-long standing and feeling helpless and silly, her mind began to wander away from the cabin and everything, and all the events that transpired over the last four days. She felt suddenly like her whole body rose up from the ground. Refusing to open her eyes for fear of breaking the illusion, Isobel sensed her body nearing the tree tops and imagined she could look down on the faun and the makeshift cabin below her.

And then it appeared.

It seemed small, insignificant, and not much larger than a soap bubble, the most miniscule flicker of a flame sitting a few feet from Redheart. She zeroed in and felt her body move toward it. Deep in the recesses of her mind, Isobel heard May's voice, no louder than a whisper, "Yes."

The blonde girl's mind reached out to the bubble, and the warmth of the heat in the palm of her hand said this was no illusion of a fire, but something very tangible. She opened her eyes and the flame rested there. As she opened her hand wider, the flame grew larger and she found that, if she thought hard enough, it would move from place to place as she pleased. Thoroughly impressed with this, the young girl waved her hands back and forth with the flame in between as though she tossed a baseball back and forth. She pushed quickly forward and the ball shot toward the trees.

Isobel concentrated and pulled the ball of flame back to her, holding it at chest height. Looking to the tops of the trees, she took a deep breath and pushed with as much force as she could muster. The flaming orb took off like a rocket, and the tops of the trees exploded in a burst of smoke and fire.

"Excellent! Now find something to put it out or the whole damned forest will burn down," Redheart crowed.

Isobel moved, stretched out her arms, and a large portion of earth began to rumble beneath them. As she raised her hands, great clods of dirt lifted from the forest floor and plodded along toward the flames when an idea planted itself firmly in the front of her brain.

The heaps of dirt dropped back to the earth and Isobel raised her hands up toward the burning tree tops. The harder she concentrated, the faster the flames pulled out of the wood and moved back toward her.

"Fight fire with fire?" Isobel said.

The bulk of the flames had left the trees, though a few branches remained alight and the tips of the swirling, burning streaks were just about to her finger tips when she felt the first drops of water. She caught an image out of the corner of her eye and with her focus gone, the flames shot back to the tops of the trees they came from. In a blink, the girl stood amid a torrential downpour, watching the burning trees getting doused in the rain. Two fauns came through the trees, one of averages size and the other, taller and entirely more graceful. The walked determinedly up her and Redheart, eyeing them both with an air of contempt.

"Fight fire with fire? It's a wonder you lot made it out of the Stone Age," Urisk said.

THIRTY-ONE

"I might have known you'd be a part of this," Dreadhorn growled.

"Maurice, and His Majesty… wait, this isn't Lucerne, who is this faun?" said Redheart.

The perfect faun strode forward and pawed at the ground as he stood face to face with Redheart.

"Faun? I am no faun. I am Urisk, I am the first and you will think yourself lucky that I haven't struck you down already," he bellowed.

"Good lord. Are you really?" Redheart gasped.

Redheart studied the bewitching, flawless faun as he began to circle him. Not in a threatening way, but clearly enraptured with the perfection that stood before him.

When he had quite enough of being eyed up like a well-marbled steak in a butcher's window, Urisk thrust his arm out and stopped the faun in his tracks.

"Who is that with Dreadhorn?" Isobel asked.

"I don't know."

"And where is the King?"

"I don't know that either,"

"Do you think that's him, Urisk?"

"I don't know," Redheart sighed.

"Shouldn't you find out?" Isobel asked.

"Who are you?" the graceful faun interrupted.

"Redheart. James Cagney Redheart," the small faun said.

"Redheart? Redheart?" the golden faun muttered.

Urisk's eyes narrowed and he felt the bitter taste of a lifetime of anger rising up from his gut.

"Charles was your father, correct?"

"How did you know?"

The statuesque proto-faun stepped back and closed his eyes, beginning a low, guttural chanting far in the back of his throat. The air around him seemed to thicken and vibrate impossibly quick, sending bits of twigs and old dried leaves into the quivering mass of air around him. Soon the air churned and swirled around the golden faun's feet. It puffed and hissed and moved onward toward the makeshift cabin, bearing down on the two figures. The wind storm continued to convulse, never ceasing its movement and growing in size and speed in a dizzying vortex of ligneous flotsam.

Isobel could feel the wind build and whip the bracken and dirt against her face and, for reasons unrevealed, stepped in front of the small faun when she saw Urisk move forward.

The perfect faun continued his single-minded progression toward the two of them, bringing the swirling mass of air perilously close to engulfing her. Urisk raised his hands chest high and smiled a virulent, knowing smile as the cyclone reached a lethal velocity and began pushing it toward the girl.

Isobel shoved her shoulder outward and braced against the impending collision with the moving wall of air as though she pushed on a heavy door, held firmly closed by the tempest. She stood in silent, awful anticipation for what seemed an eternity, and when nothing happened, turned back to face Urisk.

The marble worthy faun stood across from her, ankle deep in a pile of leaves and twigs and looking entirely vexed by what just happened. Isobel brought her hands together as though she was about to give him a round of applause and suddenly felt the heat of a small globe of flame between them.

"Thank-you." Urisk raised a hand and called the flame to him from out of Isobel's palm. "I've found I have a talent for using fire."

The first faun slowly brought his other hand forward to the flame, and when he could feel the full heat of it, pulled them apart and felt the ball grow larger. When he was satisfied with the size it had stretched to, Urisk gave a slight push forward and launched the flame ball at Isobel like a canon shot.

The burning orb careened toward the blonde-haired girl and struck her in the centre of the chest before she had time to react. Isobel flew backward and bounced off a thick poplar trunk, landing in a crumpled heap at the foot of it.

"But I never could produce it," the golden faun said.

Redheart looked at Isobel's lifeless body in mute disbelief, and turned his attention back to the other two fauns. A smug and satisfied grin slunk across Dreadhorn's face, and the little faun in the red waistcoat felt the rage start to creep its way through his veins and slam into his brain like a night of too much good wine.

"You bastard!" he screamed, and launched himself at Urisk.

Redheart made it to within inches of the larger faun's throat when a stout hoof across the left cheek, courtesy of Dreadhorn, ceased his forward momentum.

"Ugnh!"

"Oh dear, James, you seem to have fallen down," Dreadhorn said.

Redheart picked himself up and squared up against the other faun.

"You don't really mean to go through with this, do you?" Dreadhorn asked. "Don't you know who I am?"

"Yes." Redheart wiped the blood and dirt from the corners of his mouth. "You are Maurice Chevalier Dreadhorn, sergeant at arms and high protector to his majesty Lucerne III king of all fauns. Where is our king, by the way?"

"Ah yes. Well that's another matter altogether," Dreadhorn stammered.

And that was all the time he needed. Redheart leaped at the befuddled faun and kissed the bridge of his nose with as tight a fist as he could manage. Dreadhorn dropped, if only for a moment, and shot up to clamp his hands around Redheart's throat.

"Are you ready to die, cousin?" Dreadhorn squeezed for all he was worth.

"Get up girl," Urisk commanded.

Isobel opened one eye and saw, firstly, she hadn't died as a result of the assault, and her situation hadn't improved at all. She grabbed a low hanging branch and hauled herself slowly and painfully upward.

"Ah, you haven't expired. Excellent. Now here is precisely what's going to happen. I am going to go into my cabin for a moment and then I am going to return to this spot, at which point I am going to kill you."

"And? Am I to take this as a warning? I'm going to kill you if I see you past sundown type of thing?" Isobel asked.

"No, no. No warning. It was more of a statement of fact. An 'I am going to kill you and then I am going to reduce your town to ash,' type of thing."

He turned and walked past the hanging blanket into the cabin.

Isobel could hear him rooting around inside, cursing to himself, and after a few moments, he returned and stood in front of her.

"Right. Already then?" the exquisite faun asked.

"All… wait, what?"

"Are you quite prepared to die?"

"You were serious?"

"Oh, yes, my dear. I've got a great many things to do and I won't have you poking around and mucking them up. Now hold still and I will try to make this as painless as possible."

He stepped back, looking as though he might charge at her and instinctively, Isobel jerked her hands up to protect herself. In doing so, she caused roots and vines and all manner of other tendrils to erupt from the ground and snake themselves around the faun's hands and feet and neck.

"Clever girl."

Redheart pulled himself up to his full height and immediately battered into the other faun with a savage, almost mindless fury he was surprised he possessed, and soon found himself perched on Dreadhorn's chest, hammering away with fist after gruesome fist. In time, the barrage began to slow to random punches and poorly aimed slaps and eventually he stopped altogether, too exhausted to carry on.

"James. James, we don't have to do this, we're kin. Just get off me and you can leave," Dreadhorn breathed.

Redheart leaned back without getting off the other faun.

"Why?" Redheart asked.

"What?" Dreadhorn asked.

"Why should I stop? Why shouldn't I just stay on top of you and continue beating you to death?"

"We are family you and I. Doesn't that mean anything to you?" Dreadhorn said.

"We are second cousins. Twice removed on my mother's side."

"But family," Dreadhorn said hopefully.

"If I recall, my mother always told me she couldn't stand that side of the family," Redheart said.

Redheart levelled his arm, tightened his fist, and delivered a short, sharp punch to the centre of Dreadhorn's nose. The blood sprayed upward and covered much of the smaller faun's face. He cocked his arm back to deliver another gruesome blow but stopped short of delivering it when he realized the other faun had ceased defending himself.

"What?" Redheart asked.

"What, what?" Dreadhorn said.

"You've stopped fighting."

"Well, yes. Wouldn't you?" Dreadhorn said.

"What?"

"You're right, you've hit the nail on the head, along with me of course," he joked nervously. "We are family but only just, why should you want to demean yourself by listening to what I have to say, though it might make completely perfect sense?"

"Well I... What do you mean?"

The little faun in the red waist coat leaned back off of his cousin's chest and suddenly found himself feeling sorry for the faun that had attempted to kill him only moments before.

"Maurice, listen, I just want to say that..."

Dreadhorn wasted no time in taking advantage of the opportunity. As Redheart leaned back, the other faun managed to free his arms, which he fired up like a shot. A crushing blow landed on the right side of Redheart's face and dazed him long enough for Dreadhorn to gain the upper hand and snatch the small black handled knife from his cousin's belt and hold it up to his throat.

"If you won't help our future, you need to be removed from our history," Dreadhorn said.

The larger faun raised the knife and began to bring it down in a sickening arc.

"My mother always said your side of the family were all pretentious snobs."

The gleaming blade nested itself in Redheart's waistcoat seconds before being dislodged from Dreadhorn's hands by a globe-sized fire ball.

"Come on. We've got to get out of here!" Isobel shouted.

"To where?" Redheart asked.

"Winterbourne asylum. Don't ask me how, but I know what Urisk is up to, and if we don't get there before he does, he'll burn the whole damned place down."

THIRTY-TWO

Isobel took off running, scrambling to get away from the forest and Urisk as fast as she could, and onto Winterbourne Asylum. It was early Saturday morning, as nearly as she could figure, and her father would likely just be walking up the lane way to check in at the guard post to start his shift.

"Wait. I need to catch my breath," Redheart puffed.

"Aren't you part animal? Capable of amazing feats of speed?"

"Part goat. Capable of negotiating steep, rocky terrain at a reasonable pace."

"Look, you haven't got a disguise or anything have you?" she said to the little faun.

"Actually, I have."

Redheart opened the satchel slung over his shoulder and removed the neatly folded, garish outfit he had been wearing when he and Karl had gone into the asylum.

"Very becoming," she lied. "You'd better put them on."

"I've only just come out of that awful place. I'm not going back in there until you tell me why."

"I know what Urisk is after. And it's inside the asylum."

"Urisk wants revenge. Bloody and agonizing revenge," Redheart said.

"No, he doesn't. I'm pretty sure if he gets a little blood on his hands along the way, more's the better, but it isn't his reason for doing any of this," Isobel said.

"What is it, then?"

"I don't know."

Redheart sighed. "Well, that's utterly useless."

"I know what it is, I just don't know what it is. Does that make sense?"

"None at all," Redheart answered flatly.

"It's a thing. It's not some grand idea that he is fighting for, he's not trying to call fauns to his cause. It's a *thing*, a real thing that was taken away from him and he wants it back. It's about him, only about him. It always has been," she said.

"And that thing is?"

"The short answer is, I don't quite know. These are May's memories I'm living and I can feel her pushing me toward the right ones, but they aren't exactly fresh and clear. I feel like I'm looking at an old photo through a window with streaks of frost clinging to it. I can only see bits of it."

"I guess bits are better than not seeing anything," he said.

"Besides, I know somebody on the inside who might be able to help us find whatever it is."

"Funny, I was thinking the same thing," he said.

Urisk and Dreadhorn cleared the treeline, arriving at the threshold of the back property of Winterbourne Asylum. They stood in silence, marvelling at the massive building.

"Sir, I have been with you for some time now..." Dreadhorn said sheepishly.

"Yes, yes, and you will be rewarded, faithful today," Urisk said dismissively.

"Well, yes, as I was saying, I don't doubt your sincerity nor your unquenchable lust for blood," Dreadhorn continued.

"And yet there is doubt?"

"It's just that I wonder if it's occurred to you, after having been out of touch for such a lengthy spell, that the people who have wronged you are likely all long dead and gone?"

"None of that matters, not anymore," the golden faun said.

Dreadhorn stopped walking and looked around at the fading grass and the leafless trees on the grounds of the estate and tried to understand just what it was this first faun really wanted. Or why he should continue to follow him any farther than this patch of yellowing lawn.

Urisk strode casually toward the back doors of the asylum.

"Sir, shouldn't we try to be a little less conspicuous about all of this?"

"Why?"

"Hey, you two!" a slightly annoyed voice from behind them hollered.

As they turned, the two fauns saw a large man in a white uniform, whose seams were currently being pushed to their absolute limit, standing behind them and brandishing a truncheon that looked more like the stick of an all-day sucker, wrapped in his beefy hand.

With the two fauns facing him now, and the man in the ill-fitting white uniform got a good look at what he had just called out to.

"What the f–" He froze, not certain what his next move should be. "Put your hands up!" he yelped in desperation.

Urisk raised his hand palm up and blew a wisp of air at the fat man in white, the force of which rendered him instantly unconscious, hurling him fifty feet away from the large wooden doors where he landed with a resounding, dreadful thud.

"What have we to fear from them?" Urisk mocked.

The two continued on unabated through the back doors and into an average sized, white, subway tiled ante-room.

"What are we doing here? A house full of lunatics and wayward mothers seems an odd place to mete out revenge against the town that has so wronged you," Dreadhorn complained.

"My heart is in this place," Urisk whispered.

"Your…" Dreadhorn began in utter bewilderment.

"Not literally. A very long time ago, something precious to me was stolen and hidden in this place. I mean to have it back."

"I see. And, ah, how do you figure we should go about trying to find it? I suppose we might wave down one of the mad men in here and just ask, shall we?" Dreadhorn said trying to sound interested.

"No. In time it will make itself known."

"Excellent. Meanwhile, we'll just wander the halls and you can blow kisses at every human we see," the thick, muscular faun quipped.

He called out to the few random inmates passing by them, only to be predictably ignored. One smallish, solitary inmate took a very keen interest in them however, and began to walk toward the two in haste.

"My good woman, I wonder if you could help us, you see my companion seems to have lost something a very long time ago and he believes that it is… wait, you're not a–" Dreadhorn called out to her.

"You!" the old one gasped.

A smile began to take hold of the corner of Urisk's mouth, threatening to spread its way across to the other side. It stopped abruptly and began resembling the marriage of an amused smirk and a venomous sneer as if he remembered some terrible slight, real or imagined, dealt to him at the hands of this tiny, old faun. He raised his arms as if entreating her to move closer and embrace him and, for the moment, it seemed as though she might.

The giant faun's eyes narrowed and his outstretched hands began to clench into rage hardened fists as she drew closer to him. The old one closed her eyes and stretched out her own arms just as Urisk opened a fist and slapped her hard across the face, hoping to stop her progress. It had less than the desired effect and the little faun continued onward and enfolded herself around him. He pushed her off and struck her again, more forcefully, and when he saw she would not cower, would not yield to his brute force, a third, vicious slap flew at her face.

"Sir! Are you certain this is absolutely necessary?" Dreadhorn whined.

"Where is she?"

"Where is who?" the old one asked, wiping the blood from her nose.

"Oh, how very droll," Urisk sighed and another slap echoed off the little faun's face. "Are we going to go back and forth like this for long?" And another. "How would be if"–and another stiff slap–"you just tell me where the hag is right now"–and yet another loud slap–"and I promise you will not suffer... much."

"Do you find that sort of talk inspires people to want to help you?" She gurgled out a blood-soaked laugh. "The hope of a quick death?"

"It's entirely more appealing than the ghastly ordeal I have in mind if you don't tell me where she is," he said.

"Followed by death?" she asked.

"What?"

"After I tell you what you need to know and you don't let me suffer too much, the end result is an expedient death, yes?"

"Naturally."

"Well, here's the way I see it. If I tell you right now, you'll kill me ever so quickly, and if I don't, you torture and break my body and then kill me anyway. If I don't tell you during all of that, there is no possible way that I could tell you where she is after I am dead. So, I think you'd better just go ahead and torture and kill me."

"What?" Urisk asked.

"Sure, have at it and let the worms feast on my entrails and all of that," she said

"Have you gone mad? Do you really want me to kill you?"

"Actually, yes. Since I have no earthly intention of telling you anything about the hag and the girl–" May clapped a hand quickly over her mouth.

"What girl?" the golden faun asked.

"Nothing. I meant May, I meant to say May," May said trying to mask the obvious lie.

"No, you didn't. You said the girl."

The golden faun shifted purposefully to the tiny female and pressed his face to hers. "I have grown weary of this, and so I am not going to ask you anything further, my dear."

Urisk rubbed his hand tenderly along her cheek and traced a path down to her shoulder where he paused and gave her two gentle, reassuring squeezes. He smiled at her with a warmth she hadn't seen from him in too many years. The elderly faun let go an unhurried sigh, realizing her demise was, perhaps, not so imminent after all.

"He will." Urisk motioned to the faun beside him. "And he isn't as nice as I am."

A cancerous smile leeched its way across the high protector's face. "Right away, my lord."

The thick, muscular faun in black leather bracers drew his knife and ambled toward the old one.

"Dada, wait!" she blurted out.

The golden faun raised his hand, as if he were about to give a signal to move in an attack the older faun. The sergeant at arms remained still, waiting patiently for his chance to pounce When, after several exhausting minutes of standing still and staring at Urisk's arm with no release., the thick faun moved toward his leader to question the delay. Dreadhorn could see a look on Urisk's face that was a mix of fear and confusion with an ample portion of dread thrown in.

"My lord?" Dreadhorn asked.

"Ugnh!" the grunt escaped the golden faun and when he bent forward with his forehead nearly to the ground and equally, impossibly as far backward, it became apparent that the father of all fauns was no longer in control of his own actions.

"Dada?" The old one said quietly?

The elder faun turned to Dreadhorn, as much to look for an answer in his eyes, as to see what he would do next. When he shrugged his shoulders, and continued to stare at his wildly contorting leader, the Old One pushed herself up off the floor and bolted toward the door of the cell.

"Ugnh," Urisk grunted again and was driven to the floor as though a house had been placed on his back.

"Ugnh!" he pushed back against the weight and managed to regain his footing, if only temporarily.

She thought of going to him, rushing to his side and trying to assuage him of the pain that wracked his body but thought better of it knowing, deep down, the second he felt better, he would resume having Dreadhorn cut her to ribbons. She blew her father a kiss and headed out the door.

THIRTY-THREE

Karl Draper lifted the hinged counter and came out from behind the bar at Butler's. It was a little past noon, but from the light streaming in through the moth-eaten curtains concealing the front windows, or the lack of it, you would have thought it closer to twilight. He raised his wrist watch to his ear and, after determining the timepiece still functioned fully, moved to open the front door.

The barman stepped through the door and immediately found himself in the middle of a throng of people, spread out along Parker Street, all looking skyward.

"Hey," Karl said to the man in the camel-hair overcoat.

"Hey yourself," the man said.

"What's going on?"

"Search me. Do I look like astrologer to you?"

"What?" Karl asked, not remotely understanding what the man was getting at.

The man in the camel-hair overcoat shot Karl a dour look and pointed to the heavens. "Do you figure you need a flashing neon sign to point the way, or is the current spectacular event good enough to get your attention?"

The mid-November sun was set high in the firmament above Parker Street, casting a blunted, yellow glare that tried valiantly to become a picturesque day under the suffocating weight of ashen cloud cover. To the right of the sun, moving across the heavens at an unnatural pace, lay the full moon. Equally doleful and carrying on its route toward the other celestial body as though failure to do so might mean its certain doom.

"What the hell?" Karl said.

"How should I know," the man in the camel-hair overcoat answered.

Moving along a course that seemed far too quick to be natural, the moon smeared itself across the face of the sun until what little light was being transmitted from it started to disappear entirely. The shadows lengthened and crept through the crowd at street level, threatening to swallow the people standing in the middle of Parker Street in a roiling, inky blackness. With each passing inch across the pale-yellow face, the shadows grew longer and larger and seemed, to Karl, to be taking on a life of their own, sinister and malevolent and willfully squeezing the waning daylight out of every available crevice up and down the main drag. In short order, the last rays of an already dying celestial body were snuffed out entirely, and Parker Street lay in total darkness.

"It can't be," Karl breathed.

"Can't be what?" the man in the camel overcoat asked.

"Do I look like a faun to you?" Karl answered.

"Asshole," the man said.

As the moon settled in front of the blackened sun, a bright ring formed around the outside of the two of them, casting a crimson glow over the street beneath. For the first time in an entire life of living and working in Winterbourne, Karl noticed every building that lined Parker Street and every street corner for as far as he could see, etched with four alternating patterns of arcane and eldritch symbols. The etchings culminated at the intersection of Parker and Colquhoun streets, four corners all glowing brilliantly and obediently up at the corona around the coupled sun and moon. In the centre of the crossroads, directly below the traffic light and glowing twice as radiantly as the other, smaller symbols, lay a fifth sigil that resembled the letter x with four crescent moons, each inside the letter's four voids.

"Jesus!" the man in the camel overcoat said.

"I think these symbols were meant for somebody who lives a little farther south than Jesus," Karl sighed.

"Ugnh!" Urisk gasped, dropping to his knees.

"My lord?" Dreadhorn asked.

"It's nothing," the golden faun said, and began to get back to his feet. Before he could raise himself back to full height and continue on, another grievous pang sent him reeling to the wooden floor.

Dreadhorn reached to help, only to be waved off by the larger faun.

"Impudent swine," Urisk spat as he forced himself up onto a single knee and then into a sort of half squat. "Do you think I'm incapable of standing under my own potency?"

Another shot of murderous pain felled him, as if it sensed the magnificent faun's arrogance, and wanted to remind him exactly who was running things as of this moment.

"Aaagh!" he screamed and fell full to the floor, curling up on the hardwood and crumpled bits of office detritus beneath his feet, too frightened to move any farther.

"Try to find a clearing," Urisk began. "Somewhere with a view of the sky, and then come back here and tell me what you see."

"My lord?" Dreadhorn asked.

"A window, find a door. Something with a clear view of the sky," the perfect faun screeched and, after several minutes of silent, rage-filled keening, added a half-hearted, "Please."

Dreadhorn took off at a gallop, heading north from where the golden faun lay writhing on the floor. He made it out through the double doors and onto the back property of the estate. The high protector gazed upward and noticed the moon, which should have long ago set and moved out of sight, glided quickly toward the sun. Within a few minutes, the heavenly body parked itself squarely in front of its daytime counterpart and showed no signs of moving off anytime soon. And with that, the whole of Na Doireachan and Winterbourne fell into blackness, save for a thick shaft of sanguine light that streamed down from the eclipsed star. The thick faun rushed back toward Urisk and found him rolling on the tile, struggling to get up.

"Sir. The sun has been–" Dreadhorn cried.

"I… know…" Urisk panted and pushed himself over onto his palms in a half push-up position. He continued to pant and grunt and move himself up and down in mock calisthenics.

The exquisite faun didn't seem to be suffering any longer, Dreadhorn was fairly certain of that, and took the opportunity to dutifully explain everything he saw in the clearing.

"The moon seemed to be streaking across the sky, sir," he began.

"I… ungh… know," Urisk grunted.

"And it came to a rest in front of the sun and blocked all the light, such as it was anyway, from said orb."

"Yes… ungh…" the golden faun groaned. "I… ungh… know."

Urisk balled up his hands so tightly that tiny rivulets of blood trickled down from the palms. And soon began slamming them into the hardwood planks. One fist after the other, over and over again until Dreadhorn thought soon there might be nothing left of them to smash. Undaunted by this display, the thick muscled faun carried on.

"A luminous ring formed itself around the outside of the conjoined bodies, and a bright red beacon shot down from the heavens like the finger of the creator himself and landed… well, I'm not certain where exactly it landed."

Urisk moved to get himself up, slamming a fist into the floor one last time, sending shockwaves rippling out past the bottoms of the trees. He pushed upward to stand, securing one leg underneath him and then the other and, with herculean effort, grasped for something to aid in pulling his frame upward to its full height. When nothing presented itself to his hands, he put both beneath and pushed up to his haunches, remaining there until he felt confident and steady enough to complete the journey upward.

The perfect faun had grown a foot or more since the two of them left the forest, and the golden sun-kissed glow that gave his skin the appearance of a carefree beach goer on an azure sky afternoon, was gone. Replaced by an ill-fitting ash-coloured hide pockmarked and thinly covered in coarse, wiry black hair, and did little to conceal the muscles that bulged and threatened to rupture out of it. Mounds of the same repugnant black hair pushed up through the soft, curly chestnut hair that once covered his shanks and took on the appearance of grotesque blackened weeds sprouting up from dense, muscular legs.

The once awesome and majestic, ten-pointed stag horns that rose up and crowned him, now hung, barely attached, twisted and splintered beneath two gleaming black horns that curved downward from the sides of his head, and ended in sharp, tapered points just below his chin. Urisk's eyes, once proud blue eyes that had seen adulation and the adoration of untold circus goers across the countryside, had narrowed with a singular, contemptible purpose and glowed as blood red as the light from the eclipse that streamed in through the trees and surrounded him like waves of heat and flame.

The towering faun snorted and pawed at the ground like a bull maddened by the stick of a lance and the waving of a blood-soaked cape. Dreadhorn stepped forward and gazed up at the other faun, looking for something, some sense of understanding in the solid, rubicund eyes.

"My lord," the smaller faun said. "I…"

"I know!" Urisk roared.

He stood to his full, menacing height, examining every inch of himself, admiring the awesome spectacle he had become.

"And now?" Dreadhorn asked.

"Now to Redheart's son and that loathsome, human child. They are here and I mean to find them. The blood moon is nigh and I will have nothing stand in my way."

The hulking grey faun sauntered through the door and out into the hallway. To his left and right, closed doors lined the corridor that emptied into the grand foyer. He stood in front of the closed door directly to his left and grabbed the handle. The door was unlocked and, without bothering to see if anyone occupied it, Urisk walked into the room, ducking to avoid smacking his head off the top of the door frame. The room was small and sparsely furnished with only a dirty mattress on the floor and an equally filthy toilet in the far corner. The girl and her faun accomplice were not in this room and so he moved on to the room across the hall. It was identical to the first room which was identical to the third room they searched, which was the very same as the next five they looked in.

"Do you suppose we could ask someone?" Dreadhorn wondered aloud.

"What?" Urisk snapped.

"Just a thought, sir. Instead of just poking our heads in, well over two hundred doors, mightn't we ask someone if they'd seen anything strange?"

"Wait," Urisk said.

"I mean it's not as if a young girl and a goat man go strutting around a hospital everyday, is it?"

"Be quiet," the grey brute hissed and cocked his ear upward and to the left, toward the end of the hallway. "Can you hear it?"

"Sir I don't–"

"Shhh. It's there, just there," he said and pointed down the corridor. It seemed to take him, guiding him like the smell of baking guides people mindlessly toward the kitchen, and he found himself drawn into the grand foyer, followed closely by Dreadhorn. The big room was deserted but for a lone inmate, spinning endlessly in a circle only he knew the purpose of and a single guard in a chair at the far end, near the stairs.

Dale Newsome was tired. He had been forced to work a double shift, from nights right into days due to another sick call, he didn't mind the extra hours but it seemed like he was the only orderly that ever had to stay to cover the absences. Coupled with the fact that he had fought with his wife the previous morning and had been far too worked up to get anything close to a working amount of sleep. Tired didn't seem a strong enough term anymore, he was damned near out on his feet. He was so tired in fact, that when two things that resembled filthy goat-men came shuffling across the grand hall, he figured it was just too many days of too little sleep playing at an already exhausted brain.

Urisk stomped past the twirling man who remained unconcerned with anything apart from completing a perfect circle at the centre of the universe, which happened to be right where he was currently twirling.

"What the f–" Dale began.

The grey faun's hand moved like a shot and grabbed the guard in the starched white uniform around the throat, stifling the rest of what he attempted to say. With little additional effort, he hoisted the man from the chair where he sat and raised the frightened face to meet his own.

"What lies at the top of those stairs?" Urisk demanded and twisted Dale's head near to the point of snapping his neck, forcing his gaze toward the stairwell.

"Off…offices," Dale wheezed.

"Which is the furthest away from the staircase?"

Urisk loosened his grip slightly.

"The director's office. It's the biggest office up there. It was old man Winterbourne's private study when this was still his house.

Urisk flashed a beastly smile at the man in white. Dale smiled back and, for the length of time in a heartbeat, actually thought that maybe today wasn't a complete wash after all. The grey faun, however had other ideas and snatched the man's hair and pulled his head back with an astonishing force, forcing his neck into a gruesome angle. With his free hand, he took hold of the windpipe and, for a moment Dale listened as the sounds of the asylum, the noise and chaos of housing nine hundred bodies in a space designed for two hundred seemed to quiet and disappear, being replaced by the awful sound of muscle and sinew being rent from bone and blood spewing liberally from an open, pulsing wound. The guard's skin blanched as his lifeblood poured out of the jagged gash in his neck, staining his starched white uniform crimson, and he was no more.

Urisk dropped the dead man and began to climb the stairs.

"Let's go," he commanded.

"Are they up there, my lord? Is it Redheart and the girl calling to you?"

"We no longer need them and if our paths cross theirs again, you may do with them as you will."

"What? What's up the stairs that is more important than getting the two of them?" Dreadhorn asked.

"The end of mankind."

THIRTY-FOUR

"This really is going to take a very long time," Redheart complained. "Trying to find something when you haven't the foggiest idea what you're looking for is a bit like looking for hay in a haystack."

The girl staggered and took a step back, her head spinning and leaving her feeling like she might hit the floor if she didn't find something to steady herself on.

"What," Redheart asked. "What's the matter?"

"I don't know," Isobel said. "Something's happened, something really wrong has happened."

"What?"

"I feel cold," she replied. "Colder than I've ever been, like all of the heat has gone out of the world and nothing will ever be warm again."

"It is a little cool in here," the faun said. "And your clothes got wet just before we left the glade. It's no wonder you're cold, I'm sure that's it."

The girl thought about it for a moment and realized he was probably right and continued on, deeper inside the asylum and closer to finding whatever they were looking for.

"Island," Isobel said.

"What?" Redheart said.

"I can see the word island and glass. An island made of glass?"

"Very good," the faun crowed. "But what does it mean?"

"No idea," Isobel said.

The blonde haired girl and her faun companion had walked unnoticed by the staff for the most part and were completely ignored by the ones that did notice them. They stood at the mid-section of a staircase, trying to decide whether up or down was the better course of action.

"I've been to the basement," Redheart said. "And I can tell you there's nothing useful down there."

"No," Isobel said closing her eyes and looking upward. "I'm sure it's upstairs."

They walked wearily up the nearly endless steps to the fifth floor and began to wonder why no one had come along and tried to stop them or, at the very least, tried to find out what exactly they were up to. As they reached the top of the steps and rounded the corner, Isobel was struck by a feeling of having been up here before.

"Wait," she said warily and pulled the little faun off to the side of the hallway. "Peek around the corner and tell me what you see."

Redheart moved his head around the wall as inconspicuously as he could and brought it back just as quietly.

"It's a long hallway with doors on either side of it, all the way down to the end. There's a single door on the back wall."

"It's down there," Isobel said.

"So we'll just go door to door asking for it?" Redheart asked.

"I have a better idea," she said.

Isobel rubbed her hands together until a faint orange glow and little whispers of flame appeared between. She lifted them, palms upward, toward the ceiling thrusting them forward, pushing the blob of fire until it connected with a sprinkler outlet hanging above the faun's head. With a pop like a Christmas cracker, the sprinklers came to life and rain began to pour inside Winterbourne Asylum.

"Hide," she breathed.

"What?" Redheart asked.

"Hide!"

As the words left her lips, the hallway began to fill with confused, soggy people. All desperate to get away from the water and all heading directly for the two of them. Isobel noticed a small broom cupboard to the faun's right and pushed him toward it, closing the door behind them as she stepped inside. The sound of the people hurrying by and the water pelting off the worn oak floor, reminded her of warm summer rainstorms at a cottage her parents had taken her to when she had been younger and their love had been healthy. It seemed like a hundred years since she had been to that place and even longer since she had seen them. A wave of homesickness washed over her and the little girl in her suddenly just wanted to go home and be with them.

When the din beyond the door had finally subsided and she was certain everyone that was going to pass by had done so, Isobel opened the door and stepped out.

"Do you suppose the rain will stop?" she asked.

"I imagine sooner or later," Redheart said.

Cautiously the two walked down the hallway, poking their heads into every room along the way but there wasn't a single thing that screamed glass island to either of them. Room by room, the hallway seemed to lengthen as they walked on until it looked like they would never find it. The water couldn't last forever and before long, people would be returning to their offices, wondering what a little girl and her half goat travelling companion were doing traipsing around the waterlogged offices of an insane asylum in the middle of an emergency.

"One more office," Redheart said hopefully.

It was the largest room on the floor and it occupied the far corner of the end of the hallway. It was also the only office whose door had remained closed after it had been evacuated. A large metal sign, bolted on to the face of the imposing wooden door, read 'H.W.C. Stowe M.D. Director.'

Isobel reached for the knob and began to pull door open toward her.

"Wait," Redheart said.

"For what?" Isobel asked. "I don't imagine he is sitting in there in the pouring rain."

The grandiose oak door swung easily and the two of them stood in the doorway, amazed by what lay before them. The room was big, grand some would say and so much larger than any of the other offices they had been in before. Isobel was confident, after having seen the plaque on the door, that this was likely the largest single room in the whole of the facility. The walls were lined from floor to ceiling with bookshelves, overfull and vomiting out ancient, dust covered tomes of long forgotten knowledge. The room's library however, wasn't enough to distract them from the room being completely dry, not a drop of water from the sprinkler system had managed to worm its way into the room.

"This room isn't even a little wet," Redheart said. "Why is this room completely dry?"

"Why is it empty if it's dry?" Isobel added.

The two of them spent longer than they should have pondering the emptiness and dryness of the huge corner office until Redheart remembered that they were actually there to find something.

"What is it again," he said hoping to free some further memory locked in her head. "This thing we're looking for?"

"I really can't see more than glass and an island," she said.

"Still not very helpful," Redheart said.

Isobel and her faun companion began to comb through the room, poring over every dust covered inch of every dust covered volume and neither she nor Redheart came across anything remotely resembling glass or an island or even anything of interest to anyone but the director of Winterbourne.

"I'm not doubting what you've seen," Redheart said. "But are you certain about the whole island of glass thing?"

The blonde haired girl's head snapped up, slightly incensed at the faun's misgivings but, after hearing her father's voice ringing in her head, telling her to think before she said anything, she lowered her head again and swallowed a large helping of crow before she finally spoke.

"No," Isobel said. "I'm not certain about any of it. I don't know if it is an island on glass, in glass or made of glass or if it means anything at all, okay?"

The little faun in the red waistcoat walked over to the director's massive oak desk and flopped down into the high backed, leather chair behind it in defeat. He felt particularly small behind the desk, all the while watching the girl flitter and flick through stack after stack of dust covered folio in complete futility.

"This is hopeless," Redheart said, desperation dripping from his words. "We'll never find it, whatever the hell it is, and this place, this town and everything is as good as charcoal."

"Maybe," she said. "Maybe it isn't a thing after all. Maybe it's something more fragile, something that only Urisk would find important. And maybe May too, maybe if I think about it she might tell me what it is."

Isobel began opening books at random, flipping through them in frenzied earnest, hoping something in these filthy manuscripts might shed some light on whatever it was they were meant to find. She reasoned that the magnificent faun and May was at least as old as some of these books and so there might be a clue in one of them. In her mind, at least, it seemed perfectly reasonable.

Redheart began to shuffle slowly and noisily through the stacks of papers on the big oak desk, not because he thought her line of thinking would actually lead somewhere but more that he didn't want her to feel completely foolish when it yielded nothing.

And that's when the little faun noticed it. On the far corner of the big oak desk rested a large, disorganised stack of papers held firmly in place by a chunky, paperweight. Redheart picked it up to, half-heartedly examined the papers it was holding down. As he did, rolling it over in his hands, the faun could see that it wasn't a paperweight so much as it was a souvenir. A stout glass snow globe, resting on a sturdy dark, wooden pedestal, from some long ago forgotten vacation. No doubt purchased at the incessant, whiny behest of a drippy nosed human child. He turned it over and nearly dropped it as the sphere's contents came into view.

Inside the snow globe was a perfectly modeled, miniature version of a wooden roller coaster, in front of which a sign read 'The Comet' and below that, 'Coney Island, NY.'

"Do you suppose this glass island might be like a keepsake, a trinket of some kind?" he asked.

"No," she answered. "I don't see how it could be."

"Oh," he replied snidely. "Never mind then."

"Wait," she asked, looking up from the latest book she was inspecting. "Why do you ask?"

Redheart held the snow globe out to her and, as Isobel took hold of it, she felt the instant, searing crackle of electricity pushing its way up through her skin like an acid tipped bee sting. It began to glow and pulse with a hollow scarlet colour, on and off like a shoddy hotel sign and soon her hand contracted into a death grip around the globe. The suddenly petrified girl at once found herself flailing and thrashing her hands, unable to release the damnable thing, though that was all she wanted to do.

"Take it!" she screamed. "Take it out of my bastarding hands!"

James Redheart reached up and grabbed the thrumming glass ball, jerking and heaving for all he was worth until he finally wrested it away from her.

Isobel dropped to the floor in a lump.

"What the holy blue fuck was that?" Redheart asked.

Isobel looked at her companion, reeling by the pain of the snow globe and even more so by the profanity that escaped the faun's lips.

"I don't know what that was," Isobel said. "But I think it's safe to say that's what we're looking for."

"Oh that's it," a familiar voice exhaled. "And I'll take it now if you wouldn't mind."

A grey and squalid faun stood in the doorway and looked like a prime example of something the cat dragged in, but far more muscular and taller than any faun Isobel had seen. Yet, something seemed familiar about him, and even if he'd never said a word, she would have known who he was blindfolded.

"As I said, that belongs to me and I will have it. Now," Urisk said.

The abomination pointed at Redheart and curled his fingers toward him, then back to himself, again and again. The little faun, as if pushed by unseen hands, walked toward Urisk holding out the snow globe to the giant grey beast.

"Stop!" Isobel commanded. The faun kept moving.

"Stop!" she shouted, and Redheart continued his path forward.

"Stop!" the girl screamed, and ran forward to punch the little faun on the shoulder.

"Ow! What was that for?" Redheart cried.

"You were going to give him the globe," Isobel said.

"No, I wasn't, I was merely..."

"Yes, this is all well and good." Dreadhorn forced his way past the hairy, ruinous thing that was once the perfect faun. "But the fact remains that bauble does not belong to you, and the rightful owner would like it back."

"You know, you're right. This doesn't belong to me, and I would give it to him, except I have this nagging feeling that I would be damning the town and everyone in it to burn if I did," Isobel said.

"Well, there's the rub. My lord Urisk doesn't want the town," Dreadhorn said.

"What?" Isobel said, sensing the other shoe was about to drop.

"Couldn't give a monkey's nuts about the town, really. All he wants is that bothersome trinket currently in James' hand, and you, of course," the thick muscular faun said.

"Wait, what? What does he want with me?" Isobel asked.

"Your blood," the brute that resembled Urisk hissed. The annoyance raising in his voice and his patience for all of this bandying back and forth, faded rapidly. "The same blood that drove me out flows in you now."

"How could my blood do all that?" she asked.

"My child, I can look into your eyes and see eyes that have seen a thousand sunrises staring back at me. Eyes that have existed since the dawn was new, not since Mummy and Daddy began fumbling toward ecstasy in the back seat of a Tin Lizzy," the massive faun said.

"Well I…"

"You are not alone in there," Urisk said.

"What? Are you telling me I have a split personality or are you saying that my parents are not who they say they are? Just so I'm certain where this is going," Isobel said.

"Wait, what?" Urisk asked.

"So, you're not interested in the town?" Isobel asked, changing the subject, hoping for a distraction.

"Never was. Now if we could just get on with this?" the first faun answered.

Redheart, who had by now shaken away the fog from his mind, realized that giving the snow globe up would spell certain doom for his friend. He cradled it and knelt down in as defensive a position as he could manage.

"Oh James. I do wish you hadn't done that," Dreadhorn said

The muscular faun drew the black handled knife from his belt and brandished it at his cousin in the red waistcoat.

"Are you going to stab me Maurice? After all that talk about blood and kin, are you actually going to stab me?"

Urisk thrust out his arm across Dreadhorn's chest, preventing him from advancing further.

"He's absolutely right, you know. You can't just kill him. He is you kin, and family is everything," the massive faun said.

Urisk slid his hand down the arm of the faun in the leather bracers and removed the blade from his tightly clenched fist.

"There now, doesn't that feel better?" Urisk cooed.

Isobel breathed a sigh. She knew she was no match for the thick-muscled faun and dreaded the thought of facing him down to save her friend. Though she would have if it had come down to that.

"On the other hand, he is nothing to me."

Urisk quickly raised a hand and launched the knife at the little faun with a withering ferocity. The blade found its mark almost in the centre of Redheart's chest and the little faun let go a heavy sigh and dropped to one side, not completely aware of what had just happened. He propped himself up on one arm, trying desperately to get back on his feet amidst an ever-growing pool of blood and looked up to Isobel with amber eyes full of despair and betrayal. Eyes that were trying valiantly to remain open and focused on the girl but were fighting a losing battle.

"No!" Isobel screamed and ran to his side.

With his free hand, Redheart pushed the snow globe toward her.

"Take," he said.

The colour in his face, what little of it remained, seemed to move out though the top of his head, and he became an ashen and blanched version of himself. Tears welled up in his eyes and ran down his face like fat raindrops on a window pane.

The little faun pushed and struggled until finally he made it onto one side. Redheart stared at the doorway to the big office and began smiling as the faun in the black waistcoat with the fine silver watch chain walked between Urisk's thick legs. There was a faint blue glow around him as he stood, unseen by all but Redheart, hands on hips, and wearing a warm, broad and welcoming smile. He stretched out his arms as if to embrace the ebbing faun and spoke in a voice barely above a whisper that filled the room like a thunderstorm.

"The garden is waiting for you, James."

"Sor…suh…sorry," he wheezed and with a rattling, laboured exhale. James Redheart was gone.

Isobel cradled his head and tried desperately to find the words that might make her feel as though there had been some greater good served by the death of someone who had only wanted to help his people by helping her. Nothing came to her, apart from stinging, anger-fuelled tears. She grasped the snow globe from the floor in front of her and stood, howling in agony as the sparks shot from it once more. The young girl tried as hard as she could to hang on to it, but the sting of the rose lightning and odour of scorched flesh was far too overpowering. Before she could stop herself, she dropped the Coney Island bauble.

The three of them held their collective breath as the glass sphere tumbled over and over toward the floor and heaved a relieved sigh when it didn't explode into shards of wet glass and cheap plastic snowflakes.

"Grab it!" Urisk shouted at Dreadhorn.

Isobel reached out for the souvenir and felt the cool breeze of the knife that had been in Redheart's chest rip the air past the back of her hand, missing it by inches and burying itself deep into the hardwood floor. She recoiled her arm and looked up to see the giant faun walking straight toward her.

Urisk freed the knife from the floor. "Now you will die."

He took hold of the hair on top of Isobel's head and pulled it tight, and exposing her throat. Then, bringing up the knife, Urisk touched the blade to her neck and prepared to drag it across slowly.

"Wait!" Isobel cried.

"Oh, my dear, whatever for?" Urisk sighed.

The grey faun felt a sharp snap against the back of his neck and turned to see the old one holding a broken length of broomstick in her hands.

"Was that meant to stop me?" Urisk laughed.

"No, more of a distraction," the old one said.

Isobel quickly reached for the globe and hurled it to the elder faun, ignoring the sparks and painful jolts as best as she could. To her amazement, the elderly faun seemed energized by the languid crimson sparks that danced around her and weaved their way in and out of her skin. The old one closed her eyes and began to sing the bizarre, two note song Isobel first heard in the faun village.

"No!" Urisk raged. He squeezed his fists as the rage seared its way through him and he seemed to grow larger in height and girth the more he squeezed. "Do you know who I am, foolish child?"

He moved to attack the tiny faun but found he was stuck fast to the spot where he stood.

"What do you think you are you doing?" he demanded.

Isobel opened her mouth to speak and felt suddenly exhausted, as though she'd never slept before that very moment. She hadn't eaten or drank anything since the rat meat stew Dreadhorn made days ago, but felt certain she'd just been given something potent and intoxicating, and now wanted nothing more than to let it take hold.

A voice echoed in her head, a familiar and soft voice that encouraged her somnolence and made the thought of doing anything but sleeping seem like an unreasonable expectation.

"Sleep. Just let go and sleep," whispered the voice.

The girl closed her eyes, and in a breath, she floated through time and space, miles away from Winterbourne Asylum.

"What I should have done a long time ago," Isobel said, though it wasn't her voice saying the words coming out of her.

May's voice, powered through Isobel's mouth, soon began singing the oddly hypnotic, impossibly low singing along with the old one.

"Stop it! Do you know who I am?" the monstrous faun cried.

"I do. And I am sorry but you cannot stay. You don't fit in this world. You never really did." May continued singing with the elderly faun.

Urisk began to take on the soft sanguineous glow of the blazing forks of lightning and howled in agony the more it flashed. Before long, he became a translucent, coral phantom.

The first faun's face grew pale in the red light as he struggled to free himself from the bonds created by their singing. He writhed and pulled, and when he was no nearer to freeing himself, he turned his eyes to the two of them.

He pleaded to the old one, "Please. Not in there, she gave it to me so long ago and I just wanted to bring it back to her, and maybe she would let me have one more day with her. One more day of giving her newly bloomed forget-me-nots, and holding hands while I looked at the love in her eyes and never spoke a word. One more day of holding her while the sun baked our skin in open fields of long, fresh grass. One more day of listening to her talk about nothing for hours and hanging on every word, just one more day of..."

Isobel stopped singing and stepped toward Urisk.

"Stop, child!" the old one cried.

"Sing. Sing or we will never end this," May's voice said.

The elder faun resumed her song as Isobel took hold of Urisk's hands, pulling his face to hers and gazed into his eyes.

"We both deserve better, my love. Just not together."

The girl leaned in and planted a delicate kiss on the grey faun's forehead. Urisk ceased struggling against the bonds of the red light and stood quietly as Isobel sauntered back and took up her place beside the old one.

The two voices continued their earth rattling, low singing and the translucent glow surrounding the enormous faun began to change its shape and contract around him. Urisk stood motionless, head bowed as the capsule continued its decline, reducing it to little more than a small round ball of light. And when it could shrink no further, it pulsed – slowly at first, and then in rapid bursts, and began to move steadily toward the snow globe. With a bewildering flash, the illuminated ball made its way inside the snow globe which had taken on the scarlet radiance of a new tree bulb on Christmas morning.

"I'm sorry, father," the old one said.

May rushed to the tiny faun and embraced her as tears ran freely down both of their faces, and after far too short of a time, she released her child and stepped away.

"I can't stay," May said.

"I know," the old one answered.

Isobel looked around the room, suddenly very awake and very aware something big had just happened, but uncertain of what it was.

The song had ceased and whatever traces of May that lingered inside Isobel's head began to fade and disappear. Soon, all fell still inside her mind.

"I'm sorry," Isobel said. "That must have been very difficult to lock up your father that way."

The old faun looked off into the distance, to the world far beyond the young girl's head and thought long about the answer before she spoke the words.

"Gets surprisingly easier the more you do it," she said.

She looked at the glowing orb at Isobel's feet.

"You've got to get this thing out of here," the old one said.

"Where should it go?" Isobel asked.

"Back under the fountain seems as good a place as any," the elder faun answered.

"But didn't he get out of that already?"

"Yes, but that was because nobody was looking. Things will be very different once you become shepherd of Na Doireachan," the faun said.

"Wait, what? The what of what now?" the young girl asked.

"Shepherd of the fauns of Na Doireachan. Though I suppose goat herder would be a more accurate description. At any rate, somebody needs to look after the place and make sure this sort of thing doesn't happen again," the old one answered.

"I can't do that. Don't you want someone who knows what they're doing? Not somebody like me. Besides, I'm late as it is, my mother's going to kill me if I don't get home."

"You managed to imprison a living god in a souvenir from Coney Island. If that isn't someone who knows–"

"That wasn't me at all, it was May's power and yours for that matter. I was just along for the ride."

"She wouldn't have chosen you if she didn't sense you had some of it in you already."

"But my father," Isobel said.

The old one sighed. "You're going to find things have changed. Your mother and your father have both walked their own paths."

"What does that mean? Look, I have to go home. I've helped your people out and I'm glad you are all safe, but now I really must be going."

Isobel turned to leave, and the elderly faun took hold of her arm with a surprisingly firm grip.

"You can't leave. James Redheart gave his life for you and–"

"And I feel awful about it, really, I do. But he would want me to be happy, wouldn't he?"

"Yes. And that is why he made it his life's pursuit to find you. He wanted you, meant for you, to become our shepherd," the old one answered.

"But I have a life. Okay, so it's a little on the lousy side nearly all the time, but there are occasional amazing moments and I'm hoping to focus on those in the very near future. I've enjoyed spending time in your world but really, I just want to go home."

"But that's just it. The sacred grove moves at a different speed, and your kind don't adjust very well. Look at how it's already begun," the faun said.

Isobel rushed to the bathroom on the west wall of the big office and screamed at the reflection staring back at her. It was her face, especially around the eyes where it was easiest to see herself, but there were no more traces of the thirteen-year-old child. Here in the mirror was a young woman of at least ten years beyond that.

"How is this possible?"

"Time moves very slowly within the spinney. Once you entered the trees, you were touched by our time. As soon as you left, your time began to catch up to you," the old one said.

How long was I in there?" Isobel asked.

"Considerably longer than you think," the elder faun answered.

"What would happen if I stayed here?"

"Your time would eventually catch up to you fully."

"That doesn't sound so bad. I have always wanted to be older," Isobel said.

"You might get a couple of good years before the aging really started. It would be just a matter of time after that."

"A matter of time until what?" Isobel asked.

"Until you died, of course. Of old age, I should think."

Isobel's gaze shifted from floor to ceiling and back again. She supposed there wasn't really any question of what she needed to do.

"You've got to let me say good-bye to him. Please."

THIRTY-FIVE

Isobel hit the bottom of the large stone staircase at the front of Winterbourne Asylum in a hurry, and broke into a jog as she neared the gated entrance.

"Well, I haven't seen you around in a while. Everything all right at home?" the guard at the gate said.

"What do you mean?" Isobel asked.

"Your dad hasn't been into work for a few days and I heard he's been spending a lot of time in Butler's."

"What? Why?"

"Sorry Isobel," the guard said, realizing she likely had no idea what he was talking about.

"Never mind that, Dave. Tell me what you heard about my father," she shouted.

"After you disappeared, the whole town was looking for you, for a really long time. When you didn't turn up, there were whispers that your father had something to do with it, everyone figured your mother must have felt that way too because she up and left your father a few months after. Ever since then, from what I heard, your father has spent most of his time in front of the bar at Butler's inside a whisky bottle."

"What do you mean disappeared, Dave? I left my house four days ago." she asked in shock.

"Isobel, your old man said you disappeared. That was nearly a year ago,"

Dave said softly.

Isobel stepped backward, groping for something to steady herself against. Dave's words rang in her head like a stiff clout around the ears, and her mouth had the unmistakeable dryness that nearly always precludes a round of vomiting followed by full-bodied heaving. She needed to get away from the little man in the cage saying these awful things. She needed to see her father, he would make sense of all of this and he would rejoice at the life she had just been handed. "Nothing good ever happened to somebody that stayed home," he would say to her. If Butler's happened to be where he currently resided, Butler's is where she'd go to find him. She took off down the gravel driveway of the asylum and headed out to Parker Street toward the bar.

"Nope. It's no good," he said.

It seemed colder than he thought it should be for this time of year, but then again, he always felt cold lately. He dug in his pocket for the dog-eared picture and stared at it through tear-soaked, blood shot eyes. It was 5:15 p.m. and Ezra Schneider was not sleeping. Nor had he slept for more days than he could remember. He began to wonder how long a body could last without sleep before it broke down entirely. The old man smiled though tears, supposing breaking down entirely had become one of the luxuries not afforded to him any longer. He looked at his reflection in the mirror behind the bar and tried to recall the last time he actually shut his eyes and didn't see her face.

After the first month passed without her, the police came to ask him questions. A month after that, the police said he was innocent, though he had long since been damned in the eyes of the townspeople. Two weeks after that, his wife all but said the girl had been dead all along, the fault of which rested firmly on Ezra's shoulders. Two days of horrific, accusatory silence later, she walked out. A further week gone and he'd found a comfortable seat inside a bottle, deciding to stay there until madness or death took him, and he had no real preference which came first.

He fired the remnants of the urine-coloured liquid in the bottom of his glass down his throat and pushed the glass toward Mrs. Butler.

"Don't you think you've had enough?" she asked him.

"Are my eyes still open?" Ezra asked.

She turned to the rows of bottles lining the shelves behind her, searching for the one whose contents almost never saw the inside of a glass. She twisted and pulled until the cork came free, put the bottle under her nose to take a long, deep breath and decanted the liquid into a rock crystal glass that had sat on the mirrored bar almost as long as the bottle had. She pushed the tumbler toward Ezra and took a hold of his hand as he reached out for the glass.

"My husband has been gone almost ten years now. He bought this bottle the day he opened this place, and as far as I know, there has only been two drinks let out of it. One the day Karl was born and one the day my husband died."

She released his hand and the white-haired man eyed her suspiciously, while sipping at the nearly cinnamon-coloured whisky.

"I want you to finish that, and then I want you to leave."

"Are you kicking me out, Margaret?" Ezra asked incredulous.

"Yes. And no. I want you to go home and get some sleep, or go home and cut the lawn or do the dishes, paint the house, but get out of here and back into the light. I want you to go home and do something to prove to yourself that you're still alive," Mrs. Butler answered.

Ezra could feel the tears well up in his eyes and he took a long draw from the scotch to keep from blubbering in front of the woman.

"Give me a bottle to go. Please Meg," he said.

She turned her back on him, and after a moment she turned back and handed him a dust-covered pamphlet proclaiming love and forgiveness was waiting for all in the kingdom of heaven.

"Take this." Margaret handed it and the bottle to the weary man. "It'll help if you let it."

Margaret smiled at the old man as he stood and pulled on an overcoat, wishing she could do something more to chase away the awful, black cloud that hovered around him night and day. He nodded half-heartedly to Mrs. Butler with a near smile on his face and headed out the front door.

3Isobel paced over the length and breadth of two full sidewalk slabs on Parker Street across from Butler's. Over and over again she attempted to come up with the best approach for walking into a bar and telling her father she was not dead, and then trying to explain where she'd been for the better part of a year. Trying to tell him everything happened to her took place over a few days sounded like a lie, even to her.

"Time flies when you're having fun?" she said unconvincingly.

The girl decided the best way to approach it was to just tell him everything, and hope he would understand. As she stepped off the curb to cross the street, a figure emerged from the doorway of Butler's that resembled her father. The man looked tall and lean and wore the coat she and her mother had bought at Gimbel's for Christmas a couple of years ago, but he carried a shabbiness and melancholy about him now. His hair, which had been more pepper than salt, was now stark white, and he looked as though he'd been rolled up and put away wet like an old pair of wool socks.

"Dada!" she called out to him.

His head hardly moved, barely acknowledged he'd been spoken to.

"Dada!" she shouted louder and waved at him.

His head snapped up and, even from across the street, she could see his face was as haggard and blanched as his hair.

Ezra poured himself through the doorway of Butler's and onto Parker Street, shielding his eyes from the glare of the setting sun that threw its tangerine glow off the widows across the street. The white haired man toyed with the idea of pulling the coat over his head in a half-assed attempt at a sun shade but decided his standing with the community was low enough already, no need to add resident oddball to the list of reasons to be rode out of town on a rail.

Ezra looked down at the bottle of whisky in his hand and was nearly overcome by the urge to turn back inside the bar and give it to Mrs. Butler, feeling he wasn't deserving enough of a free potable such as this. The white-haired man turned up his collar and prepared to cross the street and head home, mind beginning to wander, as it always did, to Isobel, and his knees started to buckle under the weight of the guilt for telling the girl to go into the woods that day.

The old man closed both eyes and lifted his head skyward, preparing to hurl a vile and horrific curse at God and all mankind for letting him dig deeper into an already inescapable hole when a voice seemed to whisper clarity to a booze-clouded brain. It wasn't the first time her words had come to him, but there was something different about it now, something tangible, as though the girl were actually there.

"Dada!" Isobel called out.

Ezra remained motionless and unfazed. If this was a trick of his mind it seemed unnecessarily cruel, and he didn't want to give it recognition, though his heart screamed at him to look up.

"Dada!" Isobel said louder, and Ezra snapped his head up to stare down this frighteningly real hallucination.

"Isobel?" he asked. He gripped the neck of the bottle tightly with wringing hands and backed away from the street. Ezra had hallucinations before, sure, but never such convincing ones. He lowered his gaze to his feet and quickly walked away from the chilling vision.

"Dada!" she called again, but he ignored her and kept walking.

"DADA!" she screamed

Ezra stopped and looked in the direction of the voice, almost afraid to believe this could be anything but a hallucination – that the girl was really standing across Parker Street calling out to him. He walked to the curb and stood, waiting for the traffic to stop. The old man could remember the smell of Isobel's hair and the feel of her arms around his neck. The white-haired man missed his daughter and wanted nothing more than to hold on for dear life and tell her how much.

Isobel was thirteen years old the day she stepped into Seonagh's woods and had always been small, so much so that when she stepping off the curb to go to her father, caused her to nearly vanish from sight between the parallel parked Chevys. She smiled at the white-haired man as he too stepped off the curb and walked toward her, and, for a second, the world clicked and everything was without equal. It was just her and her father. She felt a tightness in her chest and thought her heart might break from the crushing love inside it, pushing to get out.

Ezra beamed at her, for a moment anyway, and in that briefest of moments, Isobel watched his head whip to the right and back again. The look on her father's face changed from the rapture of seeing the safeness of your progeny at hand, to the anguish of watching life come thundering back tortuously and taking it all away from you in a breath of smoke. The girl turned to see what seized his attention so suddenly and looked back to her father, helplessly.

The Ford pick-up barrelled along with a load of beer kegs for Butler's, and when Isobel rushed out between the two cars, the driver hardly had time to acknowledge a person just stepped onto the road, let alone stop his truck. The polished chrome bumper caught Isobel just above the knot in the belt on her bathrobe and vaulted her ten feet forward before she came to a hard stop on the cold blacktop of Parker Street.

Ezra's bottle of pity-bought whisky hit the pavement and spilled its precious contents all over the road through shards of shattered green glass.

He darted across the street and knelt beside her crumpled form. The old man cradled his daughter in arms that refused to stop trembling, kissed her forehead and tried to sound sincere when he said everything would be all right.

"Dada?" she gurgled, trying to speak through the blood that filled her throat

"Yes, my darling?"

"Dada, I'm cold."

Ezra took off the ratty black overcoat, and by the time he had it draped over her, she was gone. The old man stayed with the girl, holding her lifeless body and refusing to let anyone come near until the chief of Winterbourne's finest was forced to get Mrs. Butler to come and talk to him.

"Ezra," she said to him softly, touching his shoulder. "She's gone."

"I know," he said. His voice sounded rigid and calm though tears streaked his face.

He looked up at her, eyes crimson and heavy with fat, saline teardrops and she could see he barely hung on. One more crack in the façade and she knew he'd snap beyond all reasonable retraction.

"I can't let go, Margaret. I just got her back," he pleaded.

The ambulance attendant stepped forward and Ezra straightened his back as though he might strike out at him if he got too close. Margaret Butler brought a hand up to his shoulder and eased him back down.

"It'll be all right, Ezra," she soothed.

Ezra Schneider let go of his daughter and stood as the ambulance doors closed.

Isobel Schneider's funeral took place the following Friday. It seemed a sombre and dignified affair. "The Lord bless thee and keep thee." It was all Ezra could do to keep his mouth shut and not rage at the world and everyone in it for his little girl being gone and his being left behind. And the girl was with the old man every day in those days afterward. If he stopped to stare at the reflection in a store window her face was right there staring back, if the autumn winds picked up and rustled the dying leaves on the box elder trees, Isobel's laughter was there. It whispered inside the breeze, tickling his ears and teasing that there was something other than time without her until the end of time.

Within a month of the funeral, Ezra couldn't hear Isobel's laughter anymore, nor remember her face without looking at the tattered photo in his pocket. He awoke one morning after the best night's sleep he'd had in longer than he could remember and a year had gone by. Waking up one morning in an especially light mood, he went for a leisurely stroll around the town, stopped at Odell's liquor, and bought the most expensive bottle of whisky Odell had and headed back home.

I should look decent, Ezra thought.

The old man dressed himself in the nicest suit he owned, a blue gabardine two-piece with high-waist pants, and cleaned himself up more than he had done in years; hair combed, teeth brushed, though he imagined they might all be knocked out anyway. He wiped the dust off a pair of brown leather oxfords, tied them securely to his feet, and sat down in his favourite arm chair.

Ezra looked at the whisky bottle, giving it such reverence and holding it so gingerly that it seemed more like he was holding a holy relic, rather than the Devil's own squeezings. It was fourteen years old, the same age as she would have turned that spring, and he held it up to the light in a grand salutation to her memory. He pulled the cork and filled his glass.

"What a piece of work is man," he said to the glass, and downed it in a single gulp.

"For what we are about to receive"–Ezra raised the barrel of the revolver to his mouth–"may the Lord make us truly grateful."

He bit hard on the nickel-plated barrel and pulled the trigger.

"Shit," Ezra said to the empty room.

THIRTY-SIX

Ezra Schneider sat in the room that looked just like the living room of his house. Identical in every respect but for the impeccable cleanliness of the place. There wasn't a single cobweb in any of the corners, no dust bunnies lurking under unsuspecting pieces of furniture, and the second he finished with a dish, someone came along and cleaned it for him.

The old man took the plug from the whisky he purchased at Odell's liquor on this day so many years ago, and poured himself a generous shot of it. Bringing the glass to his lips, Ezra felt the familiar tingling along his tongue and inside his mouth in anticipation of the exquisite, amber, nectar, just as a heavy-handed knock rattled his door. He hadn't left the chair before the knock came and again and it came a third time.

"All right for shit sakes," Ezra barked at the door.

He pulled the stark white door open and there stood a Necrosite, the small dreadlocked reptilian assistants of the office of Death. Middle management and civil servants of the after-life. He didn't trust them and thought, for the most part, they were overtly violent and smelled like sour milk. For the record, the Necrosites viewed Ezra as little more than an ancient plaything the new Death had taken a liking to.

"Time to go, dear boy," the Necrosite said.

"What do you mean, time to go?" Ezra asked, confused by the Rastafarian lizard thing's statement. "Your boss told me I could hang around this place until he got sick of my face, and since I pulled his dead ass out of the fire a while back, that ain't likely to happen."

A profane smile creaked its way across the Necrosite's face as he lifted his thick, stumpy arm and held up a scrap of paper.

"What the balls is that?" Ezra asked.

"Eviction notice, I should think," he said, barely containing the glee that threatened to bubble up out of his needle-toothed gullet and force him into acts of merriment he'd never be able to live down. "It appears he wants you, well, sort of gone, you see."

Ezra took the paper from his hand and his expression changed from mildly annoyed to completely stymied as he read the letter.

Your reward is at hand, it read. He turned it over.

No, really. Just shut up and go with him, was written on the back of it.

"Look, what's this all about?" Ezra bawled.

"Overstayed your welcome, springs immediately to mind," the Necrosite chuckled.

"Seems like a lot of horse shit to me."

He began looking around the apartment, going from room to room, picking things he figured he couldn't stand to be without, until he got to wherever he was going and got himself settled. In the end, he grabbed the bottle of whisky and the nickel-plated revolver and stuffed them in a backpack.

"You won't be needing those," the Necrosite said.

"Pfft," Ezra sputtered a moist reply and slung the backpack over his shoulder. "Shows what you know."

"Look, this won't take very long, but we really must be going," the squat monstrosity said.

Ezra eyed him suspiciously.

"I could hold your hand if you'd like," the Necrosite said to him.

The old man didn't like these things but trusted Davis absolutely, and if that meant going with the scaly, little, green bastard that was good enough for him.

"All right ape shape," Ezra said. "Lead the way."

The two of them left by the back stairs of Winterbourne home. Not as elaborate looking or as long as the hand carved steps that led up to the main entrance but being made from the same green and black flecked granite, gave the impression they weren't any less expensive. They crossed the grass-covered ground at the back of the home and headed in the direction of Seonagh's woods.

"Won't be long now," the Necrosite said.

"We're going in there?"

"*You* are."

As they got closer to the forest, Ezra could see two long rows of torches leading deep into the trees and his heart began to thunder in his chest. Strictly speaking, he wasn't afraid. He couldn't die, not in the traditional sense anyway, but he was still quite capable of feeling pain. And the thought of wandering blindly down a tiki-torch lit path into the middle of a forest told him he was in for a lifetime membership in the agony of the month club, albeit a short one.

"Um…" Ezra began.

"Follow the lights. There's a good chap."

The white-haired man knelt down and took off the back pack, pulled out the bottle and pistol and, after removing the cork and taking a long pull off the bottle, replaced it in the back pack and began to follow the dimly lit path. He made it a few feet in before he stopped and took another pull off the bottle.

"Liquid courage," he said out loud, and swore he could hear laughter afterward.

Ezra walked in silence for a time, and after convincing himself he'd passed the same tree now for the third time, he stopped, took another pull off the bottle, sat down and began to shout.

"Davis, if this is some kinda joke, it isn't funny."

"It's no joke, I assure you. Stay on the path, it's just a little farther," a woman's voice said.

He got back to his feet and continued walking cautiously until he could see, off in the distance, a ring of torches around a small village. There were figures walking around in it, that much he could see, but it was still too far away to make out who they were. He quickened his pace, reasoning that if they were going to try to kill him, they would have done it already.

After ten minutes of light sprinting, he stood outside the stockade fence, wondering how he was going to get in.

"We've been waiting a very long time for you," the small faun said.

Ezra stood dumfounded, staring with mouth agape at the little half-goat man who stood in front of him.

"This way," the faun said, taking his hand and leading him toward the great fire pit at the centre of the village.

As they walked through the collection of neatly kept, small wooden dwellings, fauns of all ages, from the youngest kids to the stooped elders, poured out from behind quickly opened doors and reaching hands to touch him as he walked by. Ezra's first instinct was to start swinging, and tell them all where they could get off, but he remained silent and passive and continued on until they reached the fire pit.

"Well, we're all here now. Should we have a drink to celebrate? Yes, let's have a drink," Ezra said cheerily.

He pulled the bottle from the back pack and hoisted it to his face.

A tall figure, at least twice as tall as the fauns around it and clothed head to toe in a thick gray robe, emerged from the most elaborate of the small wooden dwellings and strode toward him at a leisurely pace. A large cowl covered the figure's face and obscured its head, making it impossible for Ezra to figure out who or what it was.

"What in the creeping Jesus is going on here?" Ezra demanded.

"I missed you," the figure said.

It was the same voice he heard in the forest, there was no mistaking it.

"Look lady, I don't know you."

"You do. We haven't seen one another in many, many years," the figure in grey said.

"I think I would remember meeting a woman in this forest, especially one walking around in her grandad's grey bathrobe."

The hooded figure began to laugh.

"What the hell is so assing funny?"

"You are, Dada," the figure said, pulling back her hood.

The whisky bottle dropped from his grasp, clanked, and gurgled out its contents against one of the large rocks surrounding the great fire pit.

It was her, there was no question in Ezra's mind. She was older, yes, but the laughter behind her eyes and the freckles across her nose all pointed to this woman being Isobel. Ezra dropped to his knees and began to sob. Isobel knelt down and embraced him as he buried his face in the dirt.

"I couldn't tell you. They barely told me," she said.

"How?" Ezra asked.

"I'm not quite sure how it works. But I know it has something to do with these trees," Isobel said.

She helped him to stand and threw her arms around his neck and he felt as though they were back there in the yard behind the house, and she was so small and needed his help to get the door to the goat pen open.

"How did you find me?" he asked.

"Your friend Davis. He stops by to help the elder ones on their way if they need it. He mentioned you were staying with him up at the big house and I asked if I could have you here," she answered.

"Well, it's settled then. Let's go. We can go back to the old place. It's still empty and we can–" Ezra beamed.

"I can't leave, Dada. All the years this place has given me will come crashing down at once, the second I step past the trees. When I agreed to be the shepherd, they told me that my life as I knew it was over. The car accident was for your benefit, to give you closure," she said bluntly.

"So why am I here, then?"

"You made a choice, walked down a dark path a very long time ago and it has led you here. Living out the rest of your days in here with me is your reward for redeeming yourself."

Isobel looked at her father. She could see he struggled with it and remained silent for a time. He let out a long sigh and finally spoke.

"I didn't like my new place too much, anyway. Too clean," he said.

Isobel beamed at Ezra.

"Nope. It's no good," she said.

She hugged him tighter than she thought possible and she heard him let out a forced breath under the weight of it. It was 8:15 p.m. and Isobel Schneider wasn't sleeping.

"It's perfect," she said.

S. A. Baker is a healthcare worker and recovering professional musician who spent eleven years touring around North America and despite popular opinion, he really does know how to smile.

From early on, he excelled at telling stories and won several local writing awards before being bitten by the rock and roll bug.

He currently lives in a small town in Ontario with his wife and two children and two of the dumbest cats that have ever drawn breath. When not writing, Mr. Baker plays bagpipes competitively (no, really) and thinks about learning to fly fish. Winterbourne is S. A. Baker's first novel and is the introductory story in the Winterbourne saga.

www.ingramcontent.com/pod-product-compliance
Lightning Source LLC
Chambersburg PA
CBHW070106260626
47160CB00004B/1349